MEETING WOLFIE
A Story about Mozart

Sabine Muir

PublishAmerica
Baltimore

At the specific preference of the author, PublishAmerica allowed this work to remain exactly as the author intended, verbatim, without editorial input.

Muir, Sabine

Meeting Wolfie :
a story about
Mozart

      FT Pbk

1778904

ISBN: 1-4241-3968-6
PUBLISHED BY PUBLISHAMERICA, LLLP
www.publishamerica.com
Baltimore

Printed in the United States of America

This novel was inspired by my admiration for Wolfgang Amadeus Mozart, the greatest composer who ever lived. He wrote a vast amount of music during his short life and achieved much more than any other composer has ever achieved in such a short time.

I have adored Mozart's music for many years and as 2006 signals the 250th anniversary of his birth, I felt I had to commemorate this in some way. The actual story is fictitious, but the facts about Mozart's life and work are all well-researched and accurate.

The Mozart family lived in Cecil Court, London for a while, then moved to the village of Chelsea on 6th August 1764, in order to benefit from its healthy air, while Mozart's father was ill. At the time, Chelsea was located 10 km outside of London – today, it is a part of the city. They resided at the Randal family's house in Five Fields Row (now 180 Ebury Street). Wolfgang wrote his first symphony (K. 16) here. After Leopold's recovery, the family returned to London and from 25th September onwards, they lived at 20 Thrift Street (later Frith Street 29).

Wolfie loved England and always wanted to return. Due to family circumstances, sadly, this never happened.

Happy Anniversary, Wolfie, and thank you for the music.
1756-1791

For my darling daughter Amy
With all my love

Prologue

Today started off like any other normal school day. So it beats me how I ended up stranded in this dark and smelly cave–goodness knows where—with a famous child composer who's been dead for well over 200 years, (but looks very much alive at this moment in time), and a wakening volcano within spitting distance. I can hear the rumblings and vibrations. It's like a giant witches' cauldron, bubbling and hissing. It could erupt any minute now and swamp the place with lava.

No, I'm not dreaming. I've pinched myself already and it hurt. Somehow I don't think my friends are going to believe me when I tell them what's been happening today.

Chapter One

OK, I admit it: I'm prone to daydreaming.

I've already had a prod in the ribs from my friend Neil, to warn me that Miss Jennings has got her beady eyes on me. She is a cunning expert at catching people out. She sort of hovers around like a bird of prey and then when you are doing something wrong she swoops down on you like a vulture on a carcass. She is seriously weird.

I'm prone to a lot of things, according to my Mum. Being accident-prone is one of them. Funny word: 'prone', when you start thinking about it. P.R.O.N.E. … But then all words sound weird if you keep saying them over and over again. Take the word 'weird' for instance. W. E.I. R. D. … Now I wonder who thought that one up?

"Matthew Walker! Pay attention. I'm not going to tell you again," a high pitched voice called out.

I quickly straightened myself up and tried to look alert.

Miss Jennings stood before me, stretching her long thin neck. Her eyebrows were drawn together and her mouth was set in a grim line.

"Well, Matthew. You've decided to join us again, have you?" she said, in a voice dripping with sarcasm.

"Yes, Miss. I mean, erm…I'm sorry Miss."

"If I catch you daydreaming once more, you'll get detention.

"Yes, Miss Jennings," I said, sounding like a sheep. From where I was sitting I could see right up her flared nostrils. She reminded me of a furious camel about to spit. I suddenly found it very hard not to burst out laughing.

Miss Jennings turned on her heels and walked back to the blackboard.

"Lucky escape," Neil whispered.

I rolled my eyes heavenwards and nodded in agreement. The school bell rang.

"Don't forget to give your parents the note about your history project. You have to start collecting your material now," the teacher shouted in her best 'sergeant-major-voice'.

"Groan," I said, pulling a face. "I hate history. It's so boring. Why do we have to know all this stuff about the past?"

"I quite like it. I'm choosing the battle of Waterloo for my project. What about you?" Neil said, with enthusiasm.

"Don't know. I'd rather do the future any day. Spaceships and unknown planets, discovering new worlds...."

"You've got that dreamy look again. You'll have to stop watching Star Trek, Matthew. It'll get you into trouble one of these days."

Neil's right, of course. But my Dad and I love watching all the old Star Trek episodes on Sky TV.

Neil came round to my house after school. When we got home, we found my mother lying on the sitting room floor, wearing a yellow tracksuit. Her face was very red and she was out of breath. I dropped my school bag on the floor and ran up to her. "Mum, are you all right?" I called out, helping her up. She panted, placing a hand on her hip and giving her left leg a little shake. "Just been for a jog," she explained. "Doing some exercises now."

"Phew, you had me worried, Mum. I thought you were having a heart attack or something."

Mrs Walker rolled her eyes heavenwards and tutted. "Silly boy."

Neil and I went into the kitchen for a drink. "Orange juice, carrot juice, grape juice or mineral water?" I asked, peering into the fridge.

"Got any coke?" Neil asked hopefully.

"Coke is bad for you," I said, imitating my mother's voice.

He settled for orange juice, like me. I rooted around in the biscuit tin and thrust it at Neil. "Oatmeal and bran cookies, wheat germ and sunflower biscuits or a muesli bar?"

"Err, no thanks," Neil screwed up his nose.

"I know. Dad says we'll be turning into rabbits soon eating all this health food. If I see another salad, I'll scream"

"We're having burgers and chips for tea," Neil said, in a teasing voice.

"Oh, shush, it's not fair. I have to wait until Saturday before I see a chip. Dad promised to take me to McDonald's after the football match. He needs a good feed, too. We often go there, but Mum doesn't know."

We went up to my room to play on my computer. Neil picked up my violin. He tried to play a tune, but only managed to make it sound like a cat in agony.

"Go on, you play something. Let's hear how good you are," Neil urged, handing me the violin.

I played a song for him. While I was playing I saw a movement outside.

"Why did you stop playing?" Neil asked.

"I saw a face at the window." I put my hand against the window and peered outside. "Whoa!" I screamed, jumping back.

Neil scrambled upright from his comfortable position on the bed and came over to have a look.

"I saw someone... a horrible face, all sort of hairy and dirty like a tramp," I gasped. "With spooky eyes."

"I can't see anyone. You're probably dreaming again."

Neil annoyed me with that remark. "No, I wasn't. Look there..." I pointed at a dark figure moving about in the bushes, his long coat flapping in the wind.

"Oh, yes. There he is," Neil admitted, in an unsteady voice.

"Let's go and tell my Mum."

We rushed down the stairs, greeted by the sound of Mozart's 40th Symphony coming from the sitting room. Bursting into the room, we found my father with his back to us, waving a ruler in the air frantically, pretending to be a conductor.

As I moved towards him, calling "Dad, come quickly," my

mother rose from the sofa where she was lying down. She was ashen faced with huge green eyes.

We both screamed.

"Mum's turned into an alien!" I called out. My heart was racing.

Dad turned down the music. "Now what?" he grumbled.

"It's Mum. She's changed. She's—" Then I realised she had a face pack on. I felt really silly. "Oh Mum, why have you got vegetables on your face? You look like a swamp creature from the Black Lagoon."

"Cucumber slices are good for your eyes," she explained, without moving her lips. "Can't really talk right now. Face pack will crack."

We heard a crashing sound. Dad had managed to knock over the vase on the table with his 'baton'.

"My carnations," Mum cried out. Lines appeared on her face as her face pack cracked at last. "Now look what you've made me do."

Suddenly she looked like she wouldn't feel out of place in a horror movie.

Dad turned off the music and faced the music, so to speak. He looked kind of sheepish, as if he'd been caught in his pyjamas on the bus. His hair was in wild disarray and his glasses were askew.

. Neil checked his watch. "I think I'd better go home now."

My parents are really embarrassing. My Mum walks around like an extra on 'The Night of the Undead', and my Dad looks like a mad professor. Great. God knows what Neil must have thought.

With all the commotion, it was too late to chase the intruder. Dad checked around outside, but there was no sign of him.

After tea, I went to my room and pondered on a subject for my history project. I made sure that my curtains were tightly drawn. I still got the shivers when I thought about that horrible face at the window. I put on my computer and fiddled around for a while. I played some games and then I surfed the net for a while trying to find an era for my project.

I found a web site about caves, so curious to find out more, I logged on. I've always liked caves and would like to go potholing one day. It was the weirdest web site. It took me through a network of caves, glittering stalagmites and stalactites. I heard music, beautiful music, the sort that Dad plays. Then suddenly a man's face filled the screen. His hypnotic eyes were a piercing blue and seemed to scan my brain. As I recognised the man, I was suddenly stuck to my seat and could not move.

I don't know what happened next. I must have fallen asleep or something, but when I woke up, I found myself inside the very same cave that I had seen on the Internet. How strange, I thought. Where was I? How did I get here? The same music was playing. I looked around. There was no one to be seen. I got up and brushed the dust off my jeans. The walls of the cave were glittering and in the distance through an opening I could see stalagmites and stalactites. The music was coming from another opening in the cave wall, so I went to investigate. I ventured down into the bowels of the caves. It was a long and steady downward path. The music sounded nearer and it echoed around the walls, a fresh tinkling sound, like champagne bubbles.

I crossed the cave and when I reached the other side, I noticed a spiral staircase, so I began my descent down the endless seeming steps. The further down I went, the mustier and stale the air became. A slimy substance covered the walls. I poked it with my finger. "Ugh," I shuddered, wiping the gunge onto my trouser leg. A rat dashed out in front of me and I nearly lost my footing. Swaying forward, I leant against the wall to save myself from falling. The horrible gunge covered both my hands now.

"What a place. I hope this is just a dream, correction: nightmare," I muttered to myself. The music was coming closer. I cocked my ears to find out from which direction it was coming. Instinct told me to turn right at the bottom of the stairs, so I did just that, then walked along the massive corridor until the music became louder.

Then I found myself in a large chamber and there, in the middle of the room, sitting at a piano-like instrument, was a boy of about ten, my own age. I gasped, as I had expected an adult to be sitting there.

The boy sat upright, his back was as straight as a candle. I watched him for a while, not wanting to frighten or disturb him.

Entranced by the music and delighted to see another human being at last, after walking for what seemed like miles, I took in the boy's appearance. He was clad in 18th century clothing: knee breeches, red velvet jacket trimmed with gold. The shirt he was wearing was stark white and had elaborate collar and cuffs. He wore a white wig with a ponytail held together with a black ribbon.

"Cool," I said softly, then cast a quick glance at my own appearance. The slimy stuff I'd wiped on my trousers had now dried in and my sweater was matted with dust. The boy must have heard me, because he stopped playing and turned his head in my direction. I looked into his startled eyes, which were the colour of Mum's delft pottery.

Chapter Two

The boy got up from his piano stool gracefully, in a fluid, well-practised manner. There was a tentative smile on his face. "Wer bist du?" he said, in a soft melodic voice.

I gazed at him, puzzled, then held up my hand. "Hi, I'm Matthew."

"Oh, you're English?"

"Yes, I am."

"How did you get here? Did someone send for you too?" he asked me.

I shrugged. "I'm not sure, really. One moment I was in my bedroom and the next moment I found myself here."

"The same thing happened to me. I was practising my music and suddenly 'pfft', I am here." He spoke good English, but with a funny accent.

"So what next? How do we get out of here? I want to go home now, I'm missing Star Trek." I was beginning to feel anxious now.

"I tried to get out yesterday, but there is nowhere to go. Not a house or a tree in sight, nothing but rocks and sand and that rumbling volcano in the distance," the boy said, rolling his R's.

"What about my parents? What about school?" I panicked.

He shook his head. "We shall have to wait and see."

I tried to put on a brave face, but felt the sting of tears threaten. Blinking a few times, I cleared my throat.

"I am Matthew. What is your name?" I asked the boy.

"My name is Wolfgang. Wolfie for short."

Wolfgang shook my hand politely, which I thought was kind of weird and grown up. I dismissed the thought, thinking that he was a foreigner and that was probably what they did where he came from. His fingers were long and thin.

"I can't tell you how nice it is to see another human being here," Wolfgang said, with a little sigh.

"What do you mean? Are there no other humans here then?" I sounded alarmed to my own ears.

"No. Well, there's Diabolus… but he is not really human."

I sat down on a stone bench and looked at him expectantly.

"So who…or what is he? What does he look like?"

Wolfie's face clouded. "He's a big hairy nasty man with long dirty fingernails. He's not very polite and he's quite smelly, too. He lives in a huge cave dwelling below. I don't know how he got to be there, but then I don't know how we got here, either." He picked a bit of fluff from his immaculate jacket. "You will meet him later."

"No, thanks. I don't think I want to. I've had enough surprises for one day."

Wolfie observed me for a moment, then asked: "Tell me, Massew, where did you get those breeches? They reach down to your feet."

I snorted with laughter because of the way he had said my name. Then I looked at his serious face. "Breeches? They're jeans. Don't you have any in your country?"

"They do not fashion them where I come from. But I will ask our tailor to cut me a pair. They would be most useful."

"Yes, well. Talking about clothes, have you been to a fancy dress party?"

Wolfie's eyebrows shot up. "I beg your pardon?"

I waved my hand. "Your clothes—"

"I always dress like this." Wolfie stuck out his chin proudly, but there was a puzzled look on his face.

"Oh. Well, why not. It's a free country, as my Dad says." I

changed the subject quickly, realising that I had somehow upset Wolfie.

"Say, you play the piano really well. I wish I could play as well as that."

His face lit up. "Thank you. But it's a harpsichord actually. I've been playing for years."

"Really? I play the guitar. Not half as good as your harpsi-whatsit, but I'm getting lessons. At school, we're learning to play the violin."

"I play the violin, too." Wolfie's face became animated and he clapped his hands together. "Zat is vonderful, now we can play music together."

Before I had the chance to say anything else, Wolfie produced a violin from behind the harpsichord and handed it to me.

"I, eh—" Hadn't told him that I wasn't very good at playing it, but there was such a look of joy on Wolfie's face that I just didn't want to burst his bubble.

He cracked his fingers and stretched them out. "So, vhat shall we play?"

"Well, do you know Mull of Kintyre? That's a song we're doing at the moment."

"Pray, who is the composer of this piece?"

"Paul McCartney, I think."

"Paul Macwho?" He shook his head. I don't think I've ever heard of him."

"You must have. He was in the Beatles. Your parents are bound to know them."

"Beetles?" He gave an involuntary shudder. "Ugh, I hate insects," he said, pulling a face.

I roared with laughter. "You're such a comedian, Wolfie."

"What about some Vivaldi?" Wolfie launched into the Four Seasons.

"Oh, yes, that's on Dad's Nigel Kennedy tape," I enthused. I could see from the look on his face that he probably hadn't heard of Nigel Kennedy either. We started playing. The first bit I managed fine, but Wolfie's musical competence soon left me by the wayside.

I tried to keep up, but he was launched into a world of his own the moment he started playing. A look of pure joy came to his face, it was almost as though he 'lived' the music. I had never heard anyone play music with such dedication before. Wolfie closed his eyes and let the music sweep over him. He was totally entranced by it. When he finally finished playing, he turned to me and said:

"Why did you stop playing?"

"I couldn't keep up with you. You know the piece so well. I'm only a beginner." I gave a little shrug.

"Hmmm. Yes. You need some more lessons. I'll teach you if you like. Here." He got up and took the violin from me. "Try holding it this way."

Wolfie started playing the violin. He could play the violin as well as the harpsichord and I was astounded.

"You see?" He handed me the instrument. "Now you try."

"I can only play the first bit without notes and we don't have the music here," I told him, fingering the violin.

"Zat is not a problem. Here, I write the music down for you."

Eagerly, he snatched up a piece of paper, picked up a quill pen, dipped it into the inkwell on top of the harpsichord, and began writing down the notes as fast as the music was played.

I looked at him in amazement. "You are really good, you know. You should do concerts when you grow up."

He stopped writing and faced me. An amused smile curled his lips. "But, Massew, I have been giving concerts for years."

"You're kidding," I said, but I knew he wasn't.

"Yes, I've been all over Europe since the age of six. I've played in palaces of emperors and kings. Why, only a while ago I played music for your very own king."

"King?" I repeated. "But we have a Queen." I felt confused now.

"Yes, of course you have a Queen, too. Queen Charlotte, wife of King George III, a most charming woman."

Alarm bells started ringing in my head. "So how come I haven't heard of you? Have you been on telly? What is your full name?"

His face fell. "Wolfgang Mozart," he replied, crestfallen. "Most people know of me."

"Hang on a minute. Mozart? THE Mozart?" I scratched my head and a nervous little laugh escaped from my mouth. "You're having me on. No, impossible. I shook my head. I thought I must be in the middle of a daydream. Then I looked at him. Wolfie looked disappointed. "But he lived in the 18th century and—" I stared at him now and felt myself go all funny, like you do when they say 'he felt the blood draining from his face'. The clothes, the accent, his exceptional talent... it all fitted.

"What's wrong? Why are you looking at me like that?" Wolfie asked anxiously. He tugged at his wig.

"Wolfie, tell me something. What year is it?"

"Why, 1767 of course," he replied, with a chuckle.

"Not where I come from," I muttered. I sank down on the cold stone bench and shook my head. "So it must be true. You are THE Mozart." I took a deep breath. "You're not going to believe this, Wolfie, but I'm from the year 2006."

He stared at me blankly for a few seconds, then started laughing. "Impossible. Preposterous."

"We learnt about you at school, you know. Your father is called Leopold, he taught you how to play. You've got an older sister, who also plays music.

"Yes, that's Maria Anna, Nannerl for short." He scratched his chin.

"You are going to be very famous, Wolfie. One of the most famous composers ever," I delighted in telling him.

"Really?" His eyes widened. "Will I be rich?"

"I can't remember that bit, I suppose so." I felt hot colour creep into my face. I didn't have the heart to tell my new-found friend that he would die young and penniless.

"My parents have got a lot of your CDs and tapes," I continued, trying to sound as cheerful as possible.

"A CD? Vat is a CD?" he asked.

"Oh, it's music reproduced on a little round disc, which you put into a CD player, which you plug in," I explained.

Wolfie sat, wide-eyed with interest, but I noticed he didn't quite follow what I was saying.

19

"Plug in? What does that mean?"

"Electricity," I told him, with a chuckle. I couldn't believe this was happening. "No, of course you don't know about that. It wasn't invented in your time. I wish I could take you home to show you."

"Tell me more about your century," Wolfie urged.

I opened my mouth to speak, but heard the sound of heavy footsteps in the corridor. Wolfie grew pale and his eyes widened with fear. "Shhh," he went, holding up his hand. "It's Diabolus. Quick, hide," he said in a raw whisper.

"Where?" I said, looking around in a panic.

"Behind the harpsichord. Hurry."

A strange smell filled the chamber. Like sulphur, I thought.

"Right. Where is he," a thunderous voice exclaimed.

"Who do you mean?" Wolfie squeaked.

"The boy I sent for, of course," he bellowed.

I trembled and the blood was rushing through my veins like traffic in the fast lane. This guy definitely didn't sound at all friendly.

"What boy?" Wolfie said bravely.

"Don't play games with me," he said, coming closer. "I want him."

Wolfie stepped back.

I closed my eyes tightly and tried to stop my teeth from chattering, afraid that Diabolus would hear them.

He pushed Wolfie aside roughly. "Get out of my way," he growled. His footsteps came nearer.

"So there you are," Diabolus bellowed.

With a shudder I realised that he must be addressing me, so I slowly opened my eyes and looked up. I wasn't prepared for the sight of him. The man had very piercing blue eyes and his nose was crooked and long and ended in a sharp point. Dark stubble covered his face and his eyebrows, which met in the middle, were so thick, that they resembled a forest plantation. His yellowing teeth were unevenly distributed in his mouth, like darts thrown in at random.

Diabolus bared them in a wicked grin. "Aha," he said fiercely. He grabbed me by the collar and pulled me to my feet, as though I were a puppet made of wood.

Play me some music," he ordered.

"I...I can't play," I heard myself squeak.

"Don't lie to me, boy," he shouted. "I've heard you play before. I've seen you." He pulled down the lower lid of his bloodshot eye.

With a start I recognised the man on my computer and at my bedroom window. My heart pounded and I swallowed hard as I picked up the violin. I cast a quick glance at Wolfie, who gave me a reassuring nod.

"I—I usually play the guitar," I said feebly, "I'm not very good at—"

"Play," Diabolus ordered.

My nervous fingers played a well-practised simple little tune. Halfway through Diabolus held up his hand. "Yes, that'll do. I'll send my son later."

Wolfie and I looked at each other, puzzled.

"You." He pointed at Wolfie with a large coarse finger.

With distaste, I noticed the dirt under his fingernails.

"You can teach my son how to play this thing here." He wagged an impatient finger at the harpsichord. Then he sniffed a few times and produced a loud sneeze. He wiped his nose with the back of his grubby hand.

I cringed.

"Teach him well. Then you will be allowed to go home. I want my son to play music as well as you," Diabolus declared, with a wicked little grin, facing Wolfie. "Then I can send him out into the world and earn me lots of money, just like your father does." He directed his last remark at Wolfie.

Wolfie looked hurt. "My father doesn't send me out to make money for him," he said, with some indignation.

"Oh, no? Then why does he do it?" Diabolus placed a hand on his hip and fixed Wolfie with a mocking glare.

"He takes me to concerts because he is proud of me. He likes to show me off."

"Don't make me laugh," he said, which was exactly what he proceeded doing.

Wolfie straightened his shoulders and looked him boldly in the eye. "I will not hear anything said against my father. He's the best father any boy could have."

Colour flooded his face and he was trembling. "And another thing, I've played music since before I could talk. What makes you think that we can teach your son anything in a short space of time?"

Diabolus' eyes were like storm clouds when he thundered out his reply. "I am in charge here. These caves are mine. What I say goes, my word is law." He slammed his clenched fist down hard on top of the harpsichord, which made a loud tinkling noise.

Wolfie winced. He hated anyone abusing a musical instrument.

The man sneered. "And who said anything about a short space of time? If it takes months, even years, so be it. I've got all the time in the world."

I gasped. "But, but what about home? When can we go home?"

"Home?" He snorted. He wants to go home," he mimicked my voice in a cruel way, then threw back his head and laughed sarcastically. He narrowed his eyes.

"This will be your home from now on. You'd better get used to it."

Tears sprang to my eyes. I swallowed hard to get rid of the lump in my throat.

Diabolus stomped out of the chamber, still laughing.

I gave an involuntary shiver.

Wolfie put a consoling hand on my shoulder. "Don't vorry, ve vill find a vay out."

I smiled at him, finding his Austrian accent endearing. "I hope so, Wolfie, I really do."

We tucked into the food Diabolus had left us. At least he wasn't going to let us starve. My Mum would have a fit if she had seen the state of Diabolus, especially his fingernails and would probably have sprayed him with disinfectant and had his living quarters fumigated. But the food, which consisted of bread, cheese and fruit, looked edible enough.

Wolfie handed me a cup of milk. "You can sleep over there, if you like." He pointed at a wooden bench in the corner.

"But that is your bench," I protested.

"It's all right. It's bigger than this one and you are taller than me."

He settled down on the smaller bench. I looked at the grubby blanket, which had seen better days. It smelled musty. I lay down on the hard bench, missing my own warm and comfortable bed. I hoped that this was just a dream and I'd wake up at any moment.

Wolfie must have read my thoughts. "We'll get used to it. Don't worry. We try to get out tomorrow."

"I hope you're right, Wolfie," I said wistfully. We chatted for a while and I told him about my family while he told me about his.

"You speak such good English, Wolfie. Where did you learn it?"

"Ha, I lived in London for fifteen months. First we lodged above a shop in Cecil Court. Then we moved to Five Fields Row *, in Chelsea. In fact, I wrote my first two symphonies there. I also stayed at an address in Thrift Street **, in Soho. They were nice lodgings, near Soho Square. I loved to play in Soho Square with my sister."

"Soho?" I said. I frowned. I had heard some strange stories about that area.

"Yes, it was a lovely area," Wolfie enthused. "I'd like to go back to London again, maybe when I'm big." His expressive eyes turned dreamy again. He yawned.

"We'd better get some sleep," I suggested.

I tossed and turned for a while, my thoughts milling around in my head. I drifted into a restless sleep. When I woke up the next morning I felt tired and stiff. Then reality dawned upon me. Wolfie was still asleep and I didn't want to disturb him. He looked so peaceful. I watched him for a while, still incredulous at how I got to be here and that I was staring at a famous composer who had been dead for over 200 years, but looked very much alive at this moment in time.

* Now known as Ebury Street
* * Now known as Frith Street.

Chapter Three

Not long after we finished eating breakfast, we heard a commotion outside the door.

"But I don't want to learn to play any ponsy music. I hate music!" a whining voice called out.

Wolfie and I looked at each other in dismay.

We heard Diabolus mutter: "Oh, shut your mouth, boy. You're going to learn and that's the end of it." He dragged his son in by the ear. The boy wriggled free and scowled. His angry eyes observed us. "These two boys will teach you, Spike." He pushed him further into the room. "I'll be back later," Diabolus grunted, making his exit.

Spike clenched his lips in anger and stared at the floor.

Wolfie broke the uneasy silence that followed. "Hello, Spike. It's nice to make your acquaintance."

Spike ignored his extended hand and stuck his chin out defiantly. He was the spitting image of his father, only he had green hair, which stuck up in the middle, Mohican-style. His face was covered in spots and he wore a safety pin through his nose. He looked about fourteen.

"Well, what're you staring at?" he said, chewing gum at the same time.

"Your father said that we have to teach you how to play—" I started, then got interrupted by Spike.

"No way! I refuse to play these stupid instruments.

He sat down and crossed his arms. His big boots made an

irritating noise as he banged them against the bench.

"Oh, well, we can't force you," I said, with a shrug.

"I only like punk music anyway," Spike said, with a menacing curl of the lip.

"Punk music?" I laughed. "That style went out years ago."

"What is this punk music, may I ask?" Wolfie enquired.

"Oh, I doubt that you would like it, Wolfie. I'll tell you about it later," I smiled. "So how come you know all about punk rock, Spike? I mean," I waved a hand around, "It's hardly a hive of activity here, is it?"

"On the Internet, of course." He did guitar-strumming impressions with his hands. "I want to play the guitar."

"Massew plays the guitar," Wolfie said, with enthusiasm. His eyes lit up. "Zat is perfect. He can teach you this punk music and I will learn it, too."

I threw him a warning look. Wolfie, I—"

Spike tried a smile, but it didn't suit his sullen face. "Yeah, that's cool. You can teach me."

I sighed. "Thanks, Wolfie."

"So when do we start?" Spike rubbed his hands.

"Ah, well, there's a problem. We don't have any guitars. So you see I won't be able to teach you."

"Oh, that's no problem, Matthew. I know how to get hold of one." Spike said.

"But how? There's nowhere around here where you can get a guitar, unless you've got a music shop tucked around the corner."

"I can get it through my Dad's transporter, of course. That's how you guys got here, see." Spike said excitedly. Then he fell silent and became beetroot red. "Whoops. Wasn't meant to tell you— " he said awkwardly. "Anyway, I'll see what I can do. See yer."

When he was out of earshot, I said: "We've got to follow him, I think we are going to get out of here after all."

We followed Spike and crept along the corridors but suddenly we heard the voice of his father in the distance, booming through the caves, so we were forced to turn around and abandon our pursuit.

When the coast was clear we headed in the direction they had gone.

"These corridors are endless." Wolfie sighed. There was a long narrow corridor, which we followed until we came to a small entrance to a cave. We sat down for a while to rest. Then Wolfie let out a scream.

"There's an enormous spider in your hair," he uttered, pointing a shaky finger in the direction of my head.

"You're not scared of spiders, are you?" I smiled, combing my fingers through my hair to dislodge it. A fat-bodied spider—the biggest I had ever seen—fell onto my lap. "Whoaaa," I yelled, jumping up and dancing about. I shuddered. "It's disgusting." The spider dropped off me and ran off, looking for a safer place to have a siesta. I leaned against a wall and it seemed to give way. Upon further investigation we stumbled upon a secret passage. There was a slow, grating sound, revealing an opening in the wall. The air inside smelled musty and dank, like a grave.

We clambered through the opening and found ourselves in a large secret chamber. My mouth fell open when I noticed a large machine in the corner of the room. It had hundreds of buttons on it.

"What is that?" Wolfie asked, in awe.

"This is it. This is what we have been looking for, Wolfie. It's that machine Spike was on about. This, my friend must be the transporter."

Wolfie eyed the object with interest. His eyes nearly popped out of their sockets. "It certainly looks impressive. Do you think it will work?"

I was too engrossed to reply. I studied the machine from all angles. I found the ON switch. And pressed it. A whirring sound filled the room.

We looked at the screen and a blurred picture appeared. We never heard the footsteps approaching.

"What are you doing here?" We both jumped. Turning round, we faced Spike.

"We—er—we were looking for you and just stumbled across this place and—" Wolfie explained falteringly.

"Yes, we were going to try and work out how to get the guitars,"

I said, "to surprise you," I added as an afterthought. I gave a nervous little laugh.

"Oh," Spike said. His features softened into a cross between a scowl and a smile. He came closer. Peering at the buttons of the machine, he said: "I tried to use the timer, but it went all funny. I must have pressed the wrong button." Spike gave the machine a kick. "Stupid thing. The only one who can work this thing is Doctor Gildenstein."

My face lit up. "Thank goodness there's someone who can help. Why didn't you tell us before? So where is he?" I let out a sigh of relief.

"Ah, well—" Spike went a little pink underneath the dirt on his face. He shifted from side to side and cleared his throat.

"He sort of—disappeared. You see, he must have been in the transporter cabin at the time when I pressed the buttons and—"

I interrupted him. "**You** made him disappear?"

"Yeah, I suppose so. Well, I didn't know the geezer was in the cabin, did I? Must've been fixing it or something." Spike snorted.

"You don't know where he'll be then?"

"No, I did press a lot of different buttons to get him back, but —" he shrugged.

We stood for a while and studied the machine with its buttons and switches. I fiddled with some of them and pressed a red button. A blurred picture appeared on the screen. I pressed the keyboard and spelled out the name Gildenstein.

A tall, thin man appeared on the screen, armed with a screwdriver. He was balding and tufts of grey hair stuck out above his ears, making him look like a wise owl.

"That's him, that's Doctor Gildenstein," Spike said excitedly. We watched on as we saw him entering the transporter cabin. Then Spike appeared on the screen and fiddled with the buttons. There was a loud bang and Doctor Gildenstein disappeared. There was a cloud of dust on the screen. A little later the cloud disappeared and a little figure sat in the transporter cabin, holding a screwdriver.

"It's Doctor Gildenstein, he's turned into a—a baby," Wolfie exclaimed. Crawling around on the screen was a happy, gurgling baby, with tufts of sandy hair above his ears. He wore a nappy. Dangling from one ear were his spectacles, which were now too large for him.

Wolfie giggled. It was a silly giggle, resembling a hyena's.

I fixed him with an angry stare and said: "It's not funny, Wolfie. How are we going to get the poor man back to normal?"

I turned to Spike, who stood with a dreamy expression on his face and his index finger up his nose. "Spike, stop that, it's disgusting," I told him.

Wolfie started giggling again. Then great big hoots of laughter sprang from his mouth.

"We're stuck here forever and all you can do is laugh." I prodded Wolfie in his side. "Compose yourself."

"Compose myself, haha. I like that. Very funny." He stopped laughing for a moment, but his eyes were still twinkling and his nose twitched.

"Sorry, Massew. I can't help it. Dr Gildenstein looked so—" another giggle, "So funny."

We listened to yet another one of Wolfie's outbursts of mirth and before I knew it, I was smiling. He slapped my back and his laughter was infectious. I began to laugh, too. Then Spike joined in.

We laughed for a good while, then, tired out by it all, faced reality and returned to our living quarters.

"What will we do now?" Wolfie said, pacing up and down like a dog with fleas. He stopped for a moment and tapped out a rhythm on the top of his harpsichord.

"We have to find Dr G. He must be around in the caves somewhere," I told Wolfie. "We'll need to get Spike on our side. He might be able to help us divert attention from his father. We'll keep pretending that we will get him a guitar to keep him sweet. He's gullable and not very bright, so that shouldn't be too difficult."

"Yes, you're right," Wolfie agreed.

Spike came for a music lesson the next morning. He was as reluctant as ever. With a bored expression on his face, he snatched up the violin and held it as one would hold a guitar. He began to strum it. "This guitar's too small," he complained.

I sneaked a look at Wolfie. He put his hand up to his mouth to hide his smile.

"You're meant to hold it like this and by the way, it's a violin, not a guitar," I told him, and placed the instrument under his chin.

"Oh, yeah, of course." He sniffed.

Wolfie showed him how it should be played and then Spike had a go. He was quite happy with the sounds he produced but they were cringe-making and set our teeth on edge. Looking pale, Wolfie turned to me and whispered: "This is hopeless. He is tone deaf."

"When he stopped playing, Spike looked at them with a half smile on his face. "Not bad, eh?"

"No," said Wolfie hesitantly, knowing that this was probably the biggest lie he had ever told.

"It'll be great if we can get a guitar for you. I think you'll prefer playing that much more than a violin. We'll need to find out where Dr G is, then try to get him back to adult size."

"Yeah, we must find him soon," Spike agreed, nodding vigorously.

"But you can't tell your father, Spike. I don't think he'd be too happy about this."

"No, besides, he'll kill me if he finds out what I've done to the machine, not to mention Doctor Gildenstein." He pulled a face and made a cut-throat gesture.

"So where do we start looking?" I said, with a sigh.

Chapter Four

We began our search for Dr Gildenstein through the vast caves. We searched every corridor, every nook and cranny of the cave dwelling, but he was nowhere to be seen. We thought he might have toddled into Diabolus' quarters, so we went to look for him there. Spike was going to be on the lookout, but had obviously failed to distract him, as we were about to find out.

"Stop right there," a baritone voice bellowed.

Startled, we looked around. There, in front of us, stood Diabolus, his lips curled in a contemptuous sneer. "You're not going anywhere. I'll see to that."

Wolfie's eyes crept to the door and he weighed up the chances of a fast escape. But Diabolus followed his gaze and laughed heartily.

"Don't even think about it, boy. You're staying right here." His large mucky hand grabbed him by the collar. He lifted Wolfie right off the ground.

"You are hurting me. Let go," Wolfie called out.

"Say please," he taunted him.

"Please."

"Please SIR," he went on, with a sneer on his face.

"Please, SIR," Wolfie uttered.

Diabolus dropped him. Wolfie's hand went to his neck and he loosened off his clothing, gasping for air.

"You two do too much creeping around for my liking. I think a spell locked in your chamber is the solution. Get on your feet, boy."

He marched us back to our chamber and when we got to the door, he pushed us into the room. He pushed Wolfie too hard, and being a lightweight, he went flying across the room. As he fell, his jacket sleeve caught a nail on the bench and ripped it.

Diabolus produced a large key from the huge bunch he had in his pocket and dangled it in front of them. "No more escapades from now on. I can't trust you." The door slammed shut, and we heard the key being turned.

Diabolus marched off and when we couldn't hear his stomping footsteps any longer, we looked at each other.

"Now what?" I said, close to tears.

Wolfie rubbed his arm, which was sore from the nail catching it.

"You're bleeding, Wolfie. Here, let me have a look at it," I said, getting down on the floor beside him.

"Bleeding?" he repeated in a little voice. He went very pale, closed his eyes and turned his head away.

"Are you all right?"

"No, I don't like blood. It makes me go all sort of—erm—how shall I say it—"

"Queasy?" I offered.

He nodded vigorously, his breathing was shallow.

"Here, I've got a clean handkerchief in my pocket." Thanks to Mum, she always made sure I took a clean hanky everywhere. I folded it as best as I could and tied it around Wolfie's wound.

Soon darkness came and we were engulfed in an eerie silence. I drifted into a fretful sleep. Morning brought no solace. Our stomachs made loud protesting noises, for all we had the night before was some leftover bread from lunchtime.

Wolfie sat up. "I can hear someone coming."

I threw down my blanket and scrambled upright.

"Matthew, Wolfie... it's me, Spike. I'm sorry about what happened. My father gets really annoyed at times."

"So we've noticed," I replied, with a little grin. "Have you got a key, Spike?"

"Sorry, no. My father's got it. There must be a spare key somewhere, I'll look around. My father says you're to be taught a lesson."

"Spike, you've got to try and find Dr G. before he comes to any harm", I urged him. My stomach made another noise, making its presence known.

"Oh, and Spike, could you please get us some food? We are starving."

"I'll do my best." Off he went.

"I am so hungry I could eat ten schnitzels with sauerkraut, followed by apfel strudel and cream."

"Sounds interesting, what is it?" I enquired.

"You don't know what a schnitzel is? You don't know what you've been missing." Wolfie said, closing his eyes and licking his lips.

"Well, you won't know what a hamburger is", I scoffed.

Wolfie opened his eyes and faced me. "Huh, of course I know what a Hamburger is, dummkopf. It's a person from Hamburg."

I giggled. "I suppose so. But it's also something you eat."

"You don't say. What is it then?"

"It's minced beef, shaped sort of round and flat, like this," I explained, with necessary gestures of the hands. You fry it with onions and you put it into a bread roll with relish or ketchup."

"That sounds nice. I wish I could try that."

"Maybe one day, who knows. Hey, I've just had an idea. I'll come back to your century and we could open a burger bar. We'd make a fortune."

"I could sit and play music for the customers. Yes, imagine, people would come for miles to try out our hamburgers," Wolfie enthused.

After a while Spike brought us some food, which we ate with relish.

"I've searched everywhere in the caves and I can't find Dr Gildenstein. He must have got out."

"Oh, no," I groaned. "We have to get out of here, so that we can look for him, but how are we going to do that?"

"I'll wait till he's asleep and steal his keys," Spike said resolutely. He left.

"It's good of Spike to do this, don't you think?" Wolfie said.

"Yes, it is", I agreed. "He's not at all bad, like his father. Sometimes I wonder how they got to live here."

Wolfie spent most of the day playing music and he composed a new sonata. I watched with fascination as he jotted down the notes as fast as they came into his head. Then we played 'I spy', but the lack of variety of items in our meagre surroundings made us give it up quite soon.

I sat on the floor, resting my back against the bench. "Wolfie, could you teach me some German words?"

"Yes, if you like. He smiled his open smile and waved his hands. "I'd be pleased to."

"What does violin mean in German?"

"Niloiv."

"Niloiv?" I repeated.

"Yes", and friend means dneirf, pianoforte means etrofonaip", Wolfie said earnestly.

I sat up straight. "Tell me more",

"Llet em erom", Wolfie suppressed a giggle.

"Llet em...what?" I wrinkled my nose. Wolfie, that doesn't sound like German".

Wolfie burst out in one of his silly laughs. "It isn't. It's backwards language. You say every word backwards. It's such fun."

"Hilarious."

"My sister and I play this all the time. It breaks up the boredom of long carriage journeys. It's our secret language. I invented a new place, called The Kingdom of Rucken, which means 'backwards' in my language." His eyes shone with pleasure. "But since you are now my friend, you can use it, too."

"Wow", I said, trying to summon up some enthusiasm.

Wolfie's face was aglow. "Your name backwards is Wehttam. Mine is Gnagflow Trazom."

I smiled. "Gnagflow...That's funny. Or it could be Eiflow for short, couldn't it?"

"Taht si thgir", Wolfie replied.

I had to think for a minute. "That is—right?"

Wolfie nodded.

"You are so bright, Wolfie. You can do it so quickly. I have to think first."

"Uoy teg desu ot ti," he replied, quick as a flash.

"You've lost me, Wolfie."

"Listen, we could fool Sulobaid."

"Diabolus? How?"

"Well, we could use backward language if we don't want him to hear what we are talking about. If we're in trouble perhaps?"

"Good thinking, Wolfie. It might come in useful one day."

I picked up the violin and played a modern tune.

Wolfie joined in on the harpsichord. He managed to create all sorts of variations on the tune and I was amazed, as he had never heard it played before that day.

"That's amazing," I said. "You only heard the tune once and you can play it already."

"But of course. I only need to hear it once, then it is all up here." He ticked his forehead with his index finger.

I shook my head in awe. "Amazing. You really are something."

"I know. I am the best child musician in the vorld," he said proudly, sticking out his chest.

"And modest, too", I went on, with a chuckle. "No, I really admire you, Wolfie."

"Thank you."

Spike returned and freed us. He assured us that his father was asleep and would be for the rest of the night. So we set out on our search for Dr Gildenstein.

Chapter Five

When we got out of the caves, I heaved a sigh of relief. We walked on, ploughing through the soft desert sand, guided by the moon and stars. After a while we were tired out, as it was hard going. We scanned the horizon for any sign of Dr G., but he was nowhere to be seen. There was a smaller hill next to the volcano, which loomed dark and menacing in the near distance. It had stopped rumbling, and just like some great big wild animal, lay sleeping. With a sense of foreboding we marched on until we got to a curiously shaped hill next to it.

"It looks like a huge Emmenthaler cheese the wrong way up," I observed.

"I hope we can eat it, then," Wolfie chuckled.

"Do you think he'll be around the hillside?" Spike enquired.

"I really hope so, because if he isn't, he's totally disappeared," I said, with a sigh. As we neared the hill, it became apparent that there was an opening in the hillside, so we ventured inside. Luckily, Spike had brought a couple of torches, so we could at least see where we were walking. We tiptoed into a great big hallway.

Wolfie had great fun with the torch. It was the first time he had ever seen one, and he kept switching it on and off, marvelling at it.

We got a real fright when we saw shadows on the wall, large grey unmoving shadows of people. I shone my torch on them, and found that they stayed just as still.

"Hello, is there anybody there?" I called out, with growing apprehension.

"They are statues," Spike said, approaching them. We walked up to the collection of statues, which were standing, lying down and there was one of a man sitting down, with his head in his hands.

Wolfie screamed. We ran up to him. "Look at this one, it's awful," he said, with a shudder of distaste.

I shone my torch onto the figure's face and winced "Ugh," I went, recoiling. "You're right, it is horrible." The grey stone face had its mouth open, as though it was screaming. Its eyes were wide in fear. "I wonder what the artist called it. 'Terror' would be appropriate," Wolfie observed.

"It's like something from a horror movie," Spike said.

We went to have a look at the other statues. They were nearly as gruesome. Slowly realisation dawned on me. A vague recollection of pictures from Miss Jennings' book sprang to mind. I froze with shock.

"What's the matter, Massew? You've gone all quiet."

"I've," I cleared my throat, "I've just realised something. These aren't statues, they are real people turned to stone by the lava from the volcano, like in Pompeii. Oh," I shuddered, "it's just awful."

"Are you sure?" Spike asked, scratching on of the statues with his long fingernail. A deposit of grey ashy material fell to the floor. "That is so gross," he uttered, wiping his finger on his shirt. He stepped back in horror, bumping into another figure, which began to wobble dangerously. He turned to stop it from falling over. When it stopped wobbling, he looked at its face. He stared in disbelief, then let out a howl, followed by sobs.

We ran to his side. "Spike, what's the matter," I urged. Spike caved in and sank to the floor, shaking and crying.

"That statue," he said, in between sobs, pointing a shaky finger towards it. "It's my mother."

The cold hand of shock enveloped us all. I took a look at her face, she was beautiful and serene, like an artists' masterpiece.

Wolfie sat down beside Spike and put his arm around him. "When did you last see her?" he asked. Spike calmed down and blew his nose loudly on a dirty looking handkerchief.

"A few months ago, when she tried to persuade my father to return home and give up his experiments. He refused, saying he would make us rich first. She just disappeared and never came back. I didn't realise she had been turned to stone. " He began to weep again.

"You'll need to let your father know," I said.

He nodded. We sat with him for a while and comforted him.

We ventured deeper into the cave. Green moss grew on the walls and we could hear water dripping in the distance, as regular as clockwork. We got higher up and the path became quite slippery, the sound of dripping water became louder, echoing around the walls. We got to the top and I gingerly looked over the edge, discovering a round lake. It wasn't very large, but the surrounding cave wall was enormously high. I shone the torch upwards and it made me feel almost dizzy. The walls were full of perfectly shaped round holes, which appeared to be corridors leading to the lake. We heard a gurgling noise, coming from the other side.

"There's Doctor Gildenstein, look up there," cried Wolfie. He was right at the other side of the lake, about 20 metres up, crawling around near the edge of the entrance.

"Oh, no, he'll fall in. How can we get to him in time?" I said. My voice cracked in panic.

"We…we'll have to go back to the bottom and find the right corridor to go up," Wolfie said hurriedly.

"Yes, let's go," I agreed.

When we got back to the hall, we ran past the figures, which stood eerily in the centre, making spooky shadows on the wall. We ran up another corridor and when we got to the top, we realised that it was the wrong one. There was no sign of the babyfied Dr. Gildenstein. Then we heard baby sounds coming from the next corridor.

"There he is, look," Wolfie pointed out. Just as we turned to go back to access the next corridor, we heard a loud splash, which echoed around the walls. The 'baby' had fallen into the water.

"Oh, no. I don't believe this. He'll drown," I said, shaking.

I moved to the edge and peeked down, before diving in to save him.

It took a few seconds before I landed into the water.

"Come on, Wolfie, it's your turn."

The words echoed around the walls. "I can't swim," he admitted, "I'll come down the other way."

"Right," I called back, as I dived under the water to search for the baby.

I swam around and around and couldn't find him. When Wolfie reappeared shining the two torches on the water, I called out: "He's disappeared completely."

"He hasn't drowned, has he?" Wolfie was aghast.

I didn't answer him, instead, I dived in again to continue my search.

Wolfie paced up and down for a while, biting his nails. He called out a few times. He felt utterly useless. Then, taking a deep breath, he jumped into the water, too. He splashed about for a while, and then suddenly felt something pulling at his feet. He tried to get back to the surface, but the force pulling him down was much stronger. He became exhausted and had to give in to the power of the water. He spiralled down into a whirlpool, which went on for what seemed like ages. He felt himself being sucked away and his body seemed limp and useless. Down and down he went. The water was relentlessly powerful and there was nothing for it but to obey its command and comply. The next thing he knew was, when he was floating, exhausted, on a gentle wave. Then he heard a familiar voice.

"Wolfie—Wolfie—Are you all right?"

His eyes opened and they began to focus on my face. "I—" he began, then he coughed and spluttered and turned to his side, water gushing from his mouth. "I came after you."

I smiled at him. "That was very brave, Wolfie, considering that you can't swim." He sat up and coughed again.

"Well," I had to do something. I thought you were drowning."

"Thanks anyway."

Wolfie touched his head, and pulled off his sodden wig. He raked his fingers through his sandy blond hair, which was damp, too.

"You look so different like that. More 21st century," I told him.

"Do I?" He chuckled. "I feel sort of naked wizout my wig." He wrung it out.

"It'll dry in no time, don't worry. How do you feel now?"

"Better. What about Doctor Gildenstein?"

"He's alive and well. Look." Wolfie followed my pointed finger. Dr Gildenstein was sitting beside a rock, studying his toes.

"Thank God that he is safe. All we need to do now is take him back and make him grow again, so that he can help us to get home." Wolfie said, wringing out his sodden jacket.

"Are you all right now?" I asked him.

"Yes, but what a fright I got when I went down into that whirlpool. I said my prayers, thinking that was the end of me."

"I know. It was really freaky." We went to rejoin Spike. I carried the wriggling baby G, as I'd started to call him, to the main entrance, where we picked up Spike. He looked ashen-faced and very subdued. We got back to our chamber before dawn. I wrapped Baby G in a blanket and he began to cry pitifully. "I expect he's hungry," I said, trying to pacify him by jogging him up and down on my knee. "The poor little mite has not been fed for ages". I found a slice of bread and gave it to him. He rewarded me with a dribbly smile, showing off two bottom teeth.

"He's happy now. Look," Wolfie said, looking pleased too. After a drink of milk from a cup he began getting sleepy and his eyes kept closing. "He's sweet. Don't you think?"

"Yes, he is. But what's that smell?" I asked.

Wolfie's nose began to twitch. "Smell? What smell?" Then it hit him. "Phew. It's awful." He screwed up his face.

I looked down at an angelic looking baby G and I realised the smell came from his nappy. "Yuk, babies are so disgusting," I said, holding my nose.

"He'll need to be changed," Wolfie said.

"Well, don't look at me." I laid him down on the bench. I tried to remember what one did when a baby needed changing. Mum sometimes babysat Aunt Jenny's baby.

"We could use this old teatowel," Wolfie offered, holding aloft a greying cloth.

"Perfect. Well, if I hold him down, can you take off his dirty nappy?" I asked Wolfie.

"Why me?" he wailed, pulling a face.

Together we managed to extract the offending nappy, somehow wash the baby and pin his new nappy on. The infant was fast asleep by the time we tucked him into a warm blanket.

Spike returned. "The coast is clear. Shall we take him to the transporter now?"

We quietly crept along the corridors and thankfully the baby did not wake up. When we got to the transporter, he began to stir. So we put him into the cabin and switched on the machine.

Feverishly I tried to work out which buttons to press to turn him into an adult again. The machine made whirring noises and lights began to flicker on the screen.

"I don't know if this will work, but I'm rewinding the video of events until we see Dr G as an adult, just before his transportation, then I'm going to try and get him back here." I wiped the beads of perspiration from my forehead as I pondered, fiddled and concentrated on the task in hand.

I must have pressed the right button, because, moments later the transporter stirred into action. With a 'zap' and a 'boom', the machine stopped whirring. With bated breath we all watched the cabin. Through the glass panel of the cabin, we could see the silhouette of an adult-sized Dr Gildenstein.

"Thank God," Wolfie breathed.

With trembling hands, I opened the cabin door.

Dr G looked around with large, wide eyes. He rubbed his forehead pensively, then looked at me.

"Hello, Doctor Gildenstein," I said, grinning happily.

He didn't answer me, but stretched his long legs out of the cabin one by one.

Wolfie approached him, offering an extended hand. He shook Dr G.'s hand enthusiastically.

"It's so nice to meet you properly at last. You're the only person in the whole world who can help us."

Dr G. looked at him with large surprised eyes. He then coughed and cleared his throat. His voice was husky when he spoke. He sounded sleepy.

"Where am I?"

"You're in the caves of Diabolus, Doctor Gildenstein. You were accidentally made small and got lost, but now you're big again and—" I tailed off. "It's a long story."

"I see," he said, still looking puzzled.

"What is this contraption then?" he asked, pointing at his own invention. We all looked at each other. "Where did you say I was?" This was the moment we realised that Dr G. had lost his memory.

Chapter Six

Dr G. stepped forward to take a closer look at his machine.

"It's the transporter you invented, sir. It's fantastic, it can take you to whichever place you want to go, past, present or future," I told him, trying to jog his memory.

"I invented that?" he said, with an incredulous look on his face.

"Yes, indeed," Wolfie said joyfully.

We watched his face for signs of recognition, but he wore the same puzzled frown. We were so disheartened.

"So I invented that machine?" He shook his head in disbelief. "I really can't remember doing that at all. Well, well."

We heard the heavy footsteps approach. It could only mean one thing.

"What's going on in here?" Diabolus boomed. "How come you two brats are out of your chamber?" His eyebrows knitted, framing a ferocious stare. "Thought you'd escape, did you?"

Spike blanched. "Dad, there's something I've got to tell you."

"Did you let them out?" he turned on Spike.

"Yes, it's all my fault, you see, I was only helping them to get the guitars. It was going to be a surprise. Matthew was going to teach me how to play. Then I accidentally changed Dr Gildenstein into a baby and we had to find him, cos he'd run off."

"Oh, shut your mouth, you little idiot. Don't you see they were trying to trick you? They want to escape." His voice became louder, making us shrink with fear.

"But you don't understand. I know where Mum went," Spike said.

Diabolus froze and his expression softened. "What do you mean? Where is she?"

"She's—she's dead," Spike said, gulping. "She must have died when the volcano erupted the last time. She's been turned to stone with the lava. We found her when we were looking for Dr Gildenstein." Tears sprang to his eyes.

This remark knocked the stuffing out of Diabolus. He sat down, head in hands and didn't speak another word. We all felt sorry for him.

Spike took his father, now a broken man, back to their quarters.

When we got out of the transporter chamber, Dr G banged his head hard on the low beams.

"Ouch," he called out, rubbing his head. He closed his eyes for a moment. When he opened them again he blinked a few times. A bump the size of an egg appeared on his forehead. He sat down on a chair and rubbed his head.

"Are you all right, Dr G? Did you hurt yourself?"

Slowly, he began to smile. "It's all becoming clearer now. I think I've regained my memory."

Relieved, we cheered. His personality had changed completely from the time we had seen him emerge, zombie-like, from the transporter cabin. We felt instantly at ease with him and sat and talked for a while. It appeared that Dr G. had not realised that Diabolus had kidnapped us. He felt angry with Diabolus for misplacing his trust, and abusing the experiment they were both working on. But Diabolus was strapped for cash and would do anything for money.

"Well, I suppose you boys will be glad to get home after all this?"

"You bet, Dr G." I felt myself blush. "Whoops, may I call you that? Gildenstein is such a mouthful."

Dr G. chuckled. "Of course you can. Dr G. Hmm. I quite like it myself." He tapped me on the head playfully.

"Dr. G. Would it be possible for me to go to Wolfie's century for a few days, just to see what it is like? Wolfie would like me to and I've got this history project to do at school." Wolfie and I looked at him expectantly.

He rubbed his chin. "Well, let's see. I suppose so. As long as you are in exactly the same place at the right time for your return to this century. We'll need to figure something out."

"Yesss," I called out merrily. Wolfie was thrilled, too.

Dr G. said he would send a message to my parents to say that I was safe and that I'd be home in a few days time.

We said goodbye to Spike and began to get ready for the transfer to Wolfie's century.

Chapter Seven

Salzburg, Austria 1767

Groggily, we stood up from where we had landed.

"Where are we?" I asked Wolfie, feeling a bit apprehensive.

Wolfie smiled, brushing the dust off his jacket. He looked around him. "We are in the Mirabell Palace Gardens, not far from my house. Come."

"Oh well, as long as we're in the right country. For one mad moment I thought that we'd end up in China or somewhere in a desert." I combed my fingers through my hair.

"Now remember, we must come back to this exact spot, Dr G. said. In six days' time you have to return right here," Wolfie pointed at the area where we had landed.

"That won't be too difficult to remember", I looked around me. "Right in the middle of an empty circular flowerbed next to the gate."

"Wait, I've got a coin," Wolfie said, taking it from his jacket pocket.

"A coin?"

"Yes, I am going to plant the coin right here, in the middle, just to be safe.

"That's a good idea." I looked at my watch. "It's nine o'clock now. I must remember to be here at six o'clock on Friday evening."

We walked along the path and I enjoyed the scenery. Right in front of us, on a hilltop, stood a large fortress. "It's so beautiful here and the air is so fresh."

"That's because we are in the hills. It's a pity that there aren't any flowers out yet. These gardens are so pretty in the summer."

The early morning mist disappeared and gave way to a few rays of weak January sunshine.

"I don't know about you, Wolfie, but I feel a little heady. It must be all that fresh air after being stuck in the caves all week.

Wolfie smiled. "Yes, I feel like that, too. But I'm also excited at seeing my family again soon." He stepped on, sure-footed and effortless on the cobbled roads, while I kept tripping over the uneven cobbles. The sound of hooves startled me and I turned round to see a carriage led by four horses going by.

"Come, it's this way," Wolfie said, leading me through a narrow street. We came to a street called Getreidegasse.

Wolfie came to a halt before a large cheerful looking house. He knocked on the door and opened it. "Home at last," he said, with mounting excitement.

A well-dressed stern looking man stood in the hallway. His face softened when he saw Wolfie.

"Wolfgang, mein liebe Wolfgang, du bist duruck," he called out. Tears stood in his eyes. He folded Wolfie into his arms and swung him round.

"Papa," Wolfie said, "Ich habe einen freund mitgebracht."

He put Wolfie down and faced me with curiosity. "Guten tag," he said, with a nod of the head.

"Mein freund ist ein Engellander," Wolfie explained.

"You are English? Forgive me. You do not understand German?"

"No, I don't sir," I replied.

"Then we must speak English. Leopold Mozart is my name. And you are?"

"Matthew Walker, sir." I said politely, feeling an awareness that his presence commanded respect. "From London," I added.

"Ah, London, we used to live there for a while, did Wolfgang tell you?"

"Yes, sir."

He turned his attentions to Wolfie. "We have been so worried about you. Where have you been? Why did you run away from us?" Leopold said, tears springing to his eyes again.

"I didn't run away, Papa. I—"

He was interrupted by the arrival of his mother. Shrieks of joy and mother's kisses followed and then we all went up the stairs into their apartment.

The Mozarts were convinced that I was a street urchin picked up by Matthew, leading him astray. I looked at the state of my clothes, well it would take a lot of convincing that I wasn't a street child, I agreed.

"Have some more strudel, Matteus," Wolfie's mother urged kindly.

"No, thank you, Mrs Mozart, I couldn't eat another bite. Wolfie was right, it is delicious," I said, dabbing my lips with the starched white napkin that lay next to my plate. They were all looking at me and I felt a bit conspicuous. "Salzburg is a lovely town."

"We must take you out in the carriage and show you round properly later," Leopold suggested.

"Yes, there's so much to see, you'll like it," Wolfie's mother agreed. Then, looking at Wolfie, whose jacket was slung over the back of the chair, she added:

"You've torn your jacket. You can't be seen out looking like this. People will talk." She poked at the tear in the material.

I looked at her towering hairdo and wondered how on earth it stayed upright. I couldn't believe the dress she was wearing, either. It was long and very wide from the waist down. It seemed to come straight out of a history book and was made from a shimmering material, which rustled as she walked. I thought of my mother wearing track suits and jeans and felt the urge to giggle. How out of place she would look in this room. It would be even funnier if she was transported wearing one of her 'alien' face packs.

Leopold broke my thoughts, by asking "I still find it hard to believe what you told me, Wolfie. I mean: kidnappers, caves, time machines—" he shook his head.

47

"But it is the truth, Papa, I swear." Wolfie was adamant.

"You didn't run away because of the pressure of your music, did you? Especially after our three-year tour of Europe. After all you've been all over Germany, the Netherlands, France, England—Was it too much for you, son?"

"No, Papa, really. I like performing. You know that. I really don't know what happened."

His mother felt his forehead. "I hope you're not coming down with anything. Frau Schmidt says there's a typhoid epidemic in the suburbs."

Typhoid, I thought, blimey. I fervently hoped I was inoculated against that. I didn't want to go home with a disease and infect the whole neighbourhood. I was too polite to enquire whether there had been any outbreaks of the plague recently.

"Mama, I am perfectly all right," Wolfie said, a trifle irritably.

She turned to me. "He's a weak child. He gets every illness that's going: scarlet fever, smallpox, rheumatism—" she shook her head wistfully. "We have to pamper him."

Wolfie and I exchanged a knowing look, as though to say 'mothers'

"Don't change the subject, Anna Maria," he told his wife sternly. "I want to find out what really happened."

"If you don't believe me, ask Matthew. He'll tell you. He says that I'll be a great composer and they still play my music in the 21st century."

Wolfie's parents looked at me intently, making me go red in the face. I cleared my throat. "Yes, it's true, honestly."

"Just look at his clothes", Wolfie said, pointing at me. "They're not from this century, are they?"

"Maybe they are just the fashion in England?" Leopold said. "The English tend to be—erm—modern."

The conversation was interrupted by the arrival of Wolfie's sister Maria Anna, who bustled through the door, wearing an elegant dress made of blue silk. She, too, like her mother, wore her hair up and had tendrils of hair tumbling down her shoulders. When she caught sight of Wolfie, her pretty face lit up and she called out: "Wolferl dearest, you're home." She flung her arms around him and sobbed "Oh, I'm so happy."

Wolfie, too, was thrilled to see her and they seemed so close. He introduced me to his sister, who was five years older than him. She seemed very pleasant.

Wolfie's mother poured more coffee into delicate porcelain cups and handed them round. Wolfie and his sister Nannerl talked animatedly and I felt a little out of place. I stole a glance around the room. It was lavishly furnished and expensive rugs lay on the wooden parquet floor, which shone and smelt of beeswax.

Wolfie looked at me and patted me on the back "I'm sorry, my friend, am I ignoring you?"

"It's all right, you two have got lots to catch up with. I really don't mind." Leopold lifted a stray strand of hair from his forehead and tucked it neatly behind his ear. He, too, was wearing a wig.

"It's time to get ready for church, there's a mass at twelve," Leopold said, consulting his pocket watch. He snapped it shut. He eyed Matthew up and down.

"Mother, have you got something suitable to wear for this young man?"

"Papa, do we have to go to church? We've only just got back," Wolfie said in a whining voice.

"All the more reason to thank the Lord for your safe return, don't you think, Wolfgang?" Leopold said sternly. "Come, Matthew, I'll show you where you can wash and change."

I felt a little in awe of Leopold. He had the air of an old fashioned headmaster about him, the sort my Dad had told me about. It was clear to see that Wolfie was brought up strictly.

Wolfie's mother gave me some of Wolfie's clothes. They were a bit tight, because Wolfie was smaller than I. When I looked into the large mirror, I felt as though I was about to take part in a pantomime as Bonnie Prince Charlie. I wore a white shirt and a lacy white neckerchief. The breeches felt a bit tight at the knee, so I loosened them a bit. There was a discreet knock at the door. "Come in," I called.

Wolfie appeared. He appraised me and nodded his head. "Yes, very becoming. It suits you. Have you tried on the jacket yet?"

I picked it up. "It's beautiful," I told him, fingering the velvet sea green jacket with rich gold embroidery on the edges and sleeves. Wolfie helped me on with it and brushed it flat with his hand. "All you need now is a wig. Mama is looking one out for you."

"A wig?" I grimaced. "Oh come on, Wolfie, you don't expect me to wear a wig, do you?"

"You will look odd if you don't wear one, like a street urchin, people will stare at you."

"I suppose you're right," I admitted with a sigh.

Half an hour later we all got into the carriage to go to church. I pulled down my wig a bit. It felt rather uncomfortable and itchy. Wolfie's mother had covered it in a white powder, which had tickled my nose. On my lap lay a tricorn hat, identical to the one Wolfie was wearing. I nervously fingered it.

"You look very smart, young man," Leopold said approvingly.

"Thank you, sir."

"Yes, he is handsome," Wolfie's mother agreed.

The carriage took off. I gripped the edge of my seat, as I nearly lost my balance and fell of it.

Nannerl giggled and opened the fan she was holding. She hid behind it.

It was a rather bumpy ride and every time the carriage turned the corner everyone leaned to the other side. Mud squelched under the wheels and splattered against the carriage.

Leopold smiled at me. "Clearly you are not used to this mode of travel."

"No sir, we have cars and buses and trains where I come from," I told him.

Leopold frowned. "Cars?"

"Yes, father, they are metal contraptions with four wheels and they run on a liquid called petrol," Wolfie said, with a triumphant smile, having remembered one of our earlier conversations.

"Hmmm," Leopold said, with the arch of one eyebrow. "My son tells me that you are a musician, too."

I went pink in the face. "Well, I'm learning, but I'm not very good. I'll never compare to Wolfie."

"Our Wolfie is very special," his mother said, putting her hand on his shoulder.

"Yes, and I'm very fortunate to have met him. They'll never believe me at school."

"It's a pity that I can't come back with you and convince them", Wolfie piped up. "I'd love to see how you live."

"I'm still not sure whether to believe you," Leopold said, with a hint of amusement on his face. He leaned forward and said to me "He's got a lively imagination."

"Matthew told me that people have actually visited the moon," Wolfie said. Sticking out his chin. "Isn't that, true, Matthew?"

"Yes, it is, as a matter of fact," I agreed.

Leopold burst out laughing. "Now that would be quite impossible. How would one get up there," he said, gesturing with his hands. I see Matthew's got a good sense of humour, too."

Wolfie sighed. "It's no use talking to them, they'll never believe it."

Leopold changed the subject. "There's a concert for the Prince Arch Bishop on Thursday. He asked if you would like to perform."

"Yes, I would," Wolfie said, with a smile.

"Matthew will enjoy that, too," Nannerl said, looking at him.

"Yes, that would be ace," I said excitedly, "I mean, yes that would be wonderful." I observed Wolfie for a moment. "Aren't you nervous?"

Wolfie chuckled. "No, I'm used to it by now, years of practise."

"He played in front of the Empress once, when he was just six," Leopold said proudly. "They blindfolded him and he still played beautifully, not a note out of place. He was still so small that they had to find the thickest book for him to sit on, so that he could reach the keys of the harpsichord. The Empress herself sat him on her lap and kissed him."

"And he had a crush on the Arch Duchess Maria Antonia," Nannerl said, teasing him. "She is a year older than him."

"Stop it, sister mine, or I shall have to tickle you," he warned, prodding her.

"He asked her to marry him," Nannerl continued, between giggles.

"I'll never live that down, will I?" His mouth curved into a smile. A mischievous twinkle appeared in his eyes. "Right, horse face, you have asked for it this time." He turned to tickle her fiercely in the sides, making her squeal with giggles until the tears ran down her face.

We all laughed.

I thought hard for a moment. "Maria Antonia?" I said, wonderingly, "The daughter of Empress Maria Theresia?"

"Yes, do you know her?" Leopold asked.

"No, but I know of her, we had a history lesson about her at school. She married King Louis XVI and became the Queen of France. She was known as Marie Antoinette, she was quite a spendthrift and—" I stopped abruptly, remembering the rest of the story.

"Go on," Leopold said.

"No, I don't think I should tell you, it might upset you."

"You simply have to tell us now," Wolfie urged, jumping up and down.

"Well, they chopped off her head in France."

There was a stunned silence. And they all stared at me in disbelief.

"Matteus, that is not a very nice thing to tell us," Wolfie's mother said, tutting.

"But it's the truth. I swear. Look, I'm sorry if I've upset you all."

"But why did they do that? What did she do that was so wrong?" Nannerl asked, in a voice constricted with tears. "She's such a lovely girl."

"I, erm, can't quite remember the exact reason now. History is not my strong point, although I've changed change my mind now. It's quite cool."

Leopold's features were set in grim lines and his wife averted her face, waving her fan frantically in front of her.

The carriage ground to a halt and I was so glad that we had arrived at the church. We got out in silence. Wolfie threw me an apologetic grimace. Wolfie and I walked behind his parents and sister. When our little procession arrived at the church entrance, Leopold turned round to face the boys and said solemnly: "I suggest we all pray for poor Maria Antonia to preserve her from all evil."

The church service was quite different from any I had ever attended, much grander and more solemn, too. The Mass was in Latin. The music was exquisite and heavenly, with a choir of boys singing in the balcony. My Dad would have loved this. I was quite under the influence of the proceedings. Wolfie observed me now and again, and gave me a broad smile. He sang along in a clear voice.

The subject of Maria Antonia was not mentioned again and from then on, I had to think twice about what I said. I didn't want to upset anyone again.

Chapter Eight

After the bumpy carriage journey back to Wolfie's house, my bottom felt quite sore. We all decanted from the carriage, and Leopold greeted a man and woman standing on the pavement. He kissed her hand with a bow and a flourish. She fluttered her eyelashes and smiled up at him, revealing two blackened front teeth.

"Gosh," I whispered, "She needs to go to the dentist."

"Wolfie, why do men kiss ladies' hands and not their cheeks, like they do in my century?"

"Because the rouge on their cheeks would turn blue," Wolfie explained.

"Hah, that makes sense." It would be rather strange to see women walking about with blue cheeks, I thought. Mind you, it would be no stranger than my mother with one of her face packs on.

I walked up the stairs to their apartment stiffly, but didn't complain. The welcoming smell of food cooking wafted over to our nostrils. I still felt a bit uneasy about earlier on and hoped that the atmosphere would lighten a bit. I sincerely hoped that they didn't think of me as someone who made sick jokes about people. We washed our hands in the bowl of warm water brought in by Sebastian, the man-servant employed by the Mozart family. He was a large jolly man with a good sense of humour and a ready smile. Then we went through to the dining room and sat down at the dining table. The floorboards creaked as Sebastian paced up and down, serving up the dinner cooked by Helga, their cook. A silver candlestick holder graced the middle of the table. I looked up at the ceiling and noticed the chandelier with real candles.

"I hope you like roast beef, Matteus," Mrs Mozart said, smiling at me. "I asked Helga to make it especially for you. We used to eat this quite often when we lived in England."

"Thank you, it is my favourite food," I said politely, tucking in gratefully. It seemed I was forgiven. I thoroughly enjoyed my meal and cleared my plate.

"Thank you, that was delicious," I said politely, adopting Wolfie's impeccable table manners.

"Ah, but there is still the pudding to come," Leopold said, wagging his index finger. He dabbed his mouth with his napkin. "See if you can tell what it is."

Sebastian cleared the plates away and brought in a pudding, round as a ball.

I looked at it, keeping a fake smile fixed to my face, trying to recognise it.

"It's a, a—" I said slowly, trying to remember.

"Yes, a plum pudding," Leopold said, clapping his hands together. "Typically English, Ja?"

"Of course. Yum," I said, trying to summon up enough enthusiasm to do it justice. Of course I had never tasted a plum pudding before and hoped that I'd like it. My mother never made puddings like this. We were lucky if we got any pudding at all. 'Too many calories' she would say.

I tried a bit. They all looked at me expectantly for the verdict. "Perfect," I declared. "Really delicious." I meant it.

After lunch we gathered in the music room. Nannerl and Wolfie played a duet on the harpsichord. They played in perfect harmony, a well-practised routine they had done for years.

"Come, Matthew, it is your turn now," Leopold waved at me and handed me Wolfie's violin.

"Oh, I don't know. I'm just an amateur compared to these two," I said, feeling colour creep to my face.

"Don't listen to him, Papa, he's good."

"I know part of a violin concerto by Beethoven, I said, looking at Leopold.

My suggestion was met by a blank look.

"Beethoven? Who's that? Do you know him, Wolfie?" he turned to face his son. Wolfie shrugged. "No, but what does it matter? Play it anyway."

I realised that I had put my foot in it again. I took the bow and started to play what I knew of the concerto. I looked at their faces from time to time. They seemed to be enjoying my efforts. It felt good to know that maybe I could convince them in a subtle manner that I was telling the truth and came from 2006, and was not a back street urchin. When I finished, everybody clapped.

Leopold rubbed his nose thoughtfully. "Not bad, not bad at all", he said. "Beethoven eh? I'll have to remember that name." He intended to check it out for himself. He would ask around if anyone knew of him.

"He was a very famous composer. I don't exactly know where he lived, but he spoke German."

"Did he now?" Leopold frowned. That narrowed the field down a bit. It wouldn't take him long to find out. What Leopold didn't know was that Beethoven had at that time not even been born. He would be born in 1770.

"What is his full name?" Leopold asked shrewdly.

"Ludwig van Beethoven," I told him confidently. His grandfather was from Flanders, but they settled in Germany.

"Do you know any works by him?" Nannerl asked.

"Well, there's all his symphonies, of course. He wrote nine. My father's got the whole collection on disc. He also wrote other things. His Fifth Symphony is his most famous one. It starts like this:" I put down the violin carefully on the seat and walked over to the harpsichord. Wolfie moved over to let me sit beside him. I started to play the opening bars of the Fifth Symphony. "Du du du dum…du du du dum…." I looked around for signs of recognition, but their faces were all blank. I played on, rather slowly, because I'm not a very accomplished pianist. Now and again I played the wrong note and had to correct myself.

"Well" said Leopold, shaking his head. "I'm amazed. A talent like Beethoven and I've never even heard of the chap. Well, well."

Wolfie winked at me. It seemed as though I was close in convincing him. We went to his room and he showed me some of the presents he had received when he was touring Europe.

"This snuff box was presented to me by King Louis XV, it was stuffed with money," he enthused.

"It looks like it's made of gold," I said.

"Yes, it is. Good, ja?"

I put it back on the mantelpiece and my eye caught the two crossed swords hanging on the wall.

"More presents," he said. "One from Flanders, the other from Germany."

"Do you use them at all? I mean do you play with them?"

"No, my parents won't let me in case I hurt myself, but I'm allowed to wear one if it's a special concert."

There was a faint knock on the door. It was Nannerl. "Can I come in?" she asked.

"Yes, of course," Wolfie said, opening the door.

She came into the room and the material of her dress made a swishing sound. I thought she was quite pretty, in an odd sort of way. Odd in the way that I wasn't used to seeing girls dressed up like that. She had changed wigs, and the one she wore now had corkscrew curls covering her ears. It was still high and piled up at the top, but held together with a nice pink satin ribbon. I compared her to the girls back home. They were so different to girls in Wolfie's era. Most 16-year olds I knew were going through awkward phases and did not even notice boys my age. Or if they did, just thought we were nuisances. Like Neil's older sister, she was a lazy, spoilt horror of a girl, who never helped with dishes, never tidied her room and ignored her brother altogether.

"What are you thinking about, Matthew?" she asked.

"Oh…nothing really," I said, with a little shrug.

"I think Papa is confused about what happened to you, boys," she said.

"But do you believe us, Nannerl?" Wolfie asked.

She sat down on a beautifully embroidered chair "Yes I do, but you must tell me the whole story, right from the start," she urged.

Wolfie and I looked at each other and smiled. Then we both told her our story, in turn, starting from the time that we had arrived in the caves of Diabolus. She listened with wide-eyed interest.

That evening at the supper table, Leopold said: "I saw the court composer this afternoon. He told me he had not heard of this composer called Beethoven, but he knew of a man called Beethoven, who is currently Court Singer to the Elector at Bonn, in Germany. His father held the position before him. He came over from Flanders. There are no other Beethoven's in the country, so I suppose it might just be possible that the man in question is to be a descendant of his."

"So if this fellow is to have a son called Ludwig, we'll know he's the one, right, Papa?" Wolfie patted me on the back. Triumphantly, he said: "I told you, didn't I. We wouldn't lie to you, Papa."

The candles flickered, casting a soft glow around the room. It felt like Christmas. "I think you should go to bed now, boys. It's been a long day," Wolfie's mother suggested. "I'll get Sebastian to heat you some water for a wash." She rose from the table.

I began to yawn as soon as I heard the word 'bed'. We had been up quite early that morning. I washed in candlelight. Sebastian had put out a night shirt for me, together with matching night cap. I pulled it on, thinking I may as well look the part. I glanced in the mirror. "Wee Willie Winkie," I said, smiling to myself. If only Neil could see me now, he'd have a fit laughing. I crept into the spare bed next to Wolfie's. It was so soft and comfortable. Almost immediately, I fell into a restful sleep, not even hearing Wolfie come into the room.

I woke up quite early the next morning. Birds were twittering outside and a ray of sunshine fell through the gap in the heavy sea green curtains. I looked at my watch, it was 7.15. I looked at Wolfie. The rhythmic heaving of his chest indicated that he was still fast asleep. I threw back the bedcovers and tiptoed to the window to take a look outside. I saw a bread seller with a basket of bread strapped to his back, then watched as two men walked past carrying a Sedan chair. I'd once seen one used on TV, in a historical series. Behind them, a skinny brown dog sniffed around, in search of food. The snow-capped hills in the distance looked beautiful.

I rubbed my eyes. What a different world from the one I was used to, I thought. I felt secure in the knowledge that I would be home on Friday night, back in my own home with my own parents, my computer, TV (I'd already missed two episodes of Star Trek already, so I hoped my Dad had taped them for me). But in the meantime, I intended to enjoy my stay in Salzburg.

Wolfie stirred and muttered something in German. I went to sit on the edge of his bed. "Hi," I said.

"Good morning," Wolfie muttered, yawning and stretching.

"It's lovely outside. What shall we do today?" I said keenly. Wolfie struggled upright, yawning again. "Give me a chance to wake up first." He scratched his hair, which now stood on edge like a hedgehog's spikes. He got up and padded to the door, opened it and picked up two jugs of water, which had been placed there by Sebastian. He put one on his dressing table and the other on a little wash table next to the window.

"I slept like a log, it's so nice to be back in a decent bed," I said. "I just woke up early, excitement, I suppose. Did you sleep well?"

"Hmmm," Wolfie went, before splashing water on his face.

After breakfast, Wolfie took me for a walk to show me the most panoramic views of the town. He told me the names of some of the hills framing the town, the Monchsberg, meaning the monk's mountain, and the Kapuzinerberg. He pointed out the main buildings of the town, some with their weathered green copper domes, and the Mirabell Palace. Salzburg was a beautiful Baroque town with graceful squares, and courtyards, elegant gardens and statues. I drank in the scenery, and tried to make a mental note of everything for my project. We walked along the Salsach River, which cut the town in two. We paused for a while, and watched the water flow. "There are so many churches and monasteries. People here must be very religious," I observed, shielding my eyes from the sun with my hand.

Wolfie didn't hear me. He was humming a tune to himself and tapping out the rhythm on the railing along the riverside. When we walked on, Wolfie did so with a spring in his step. His mind was elsewhere.

"You look pleased with yourself," I told him.

"Me? Oh, I've just made up a tune. I'll be able to play it at the concert on Thursday."

"Won't you need to write it down somewhere, before you forget it?"

"No, I'll remember it", he said confidently. A carriage went by, pulled by four horses. People were sitting at the back of it, clinging on for dear life every time the carriage turned into another street. They held on to their luggage, which was piled up high.

"Look at them, they'll fall off if they're not careful," I said.

Wolfie smiled. "They're on what we call 'the cheap seats', it's at your own risk, of course. We turned into a narrow street. "Come, I'll take you to the market."

A pungent smell of boiled cabbage hung sourly in the air. I tripped on the cobbles and fell. "Ouch!," I rubbed my knee.

"Is it sore?" Wolfie enquired, pulling me up.

I loosened the clasps on the knee breeches. "A bit.".

"It's bleeding," Wolfie exclaimed, turning pale. "That reminds me: Mama's got the doctor coming round today. She's having leeches applied."

"Leeches? Yuk. What for?" I said, with a grimace of distaste.

"They extract bad blood and make you feel better if you're ailing."

The very thought made me feel itchy. I tried to imagine leeches crawling over my body, sucking my blood. "That's so gruesome. Sick."

"I know. I think so, too. I usually faint when the doctor puts them on me." He gave an involuntary shudder.

As we walked along a narrow alleyway, a woman threw a bowl

of dirty water out of a side window, narrowly missing us. We ran on, laughing.

"Papa once got drenched that way."

"Really?"

"Yes, when he got home there were bits of boiled cabbage dangling in his hair. It was such a funny sight," Wolfie said, giving a hoot of laughter. "He was not amused."

I could just imagine Leopold walking around with cabbage in his hair, the thought was so amusing, that I joined in the laughter all the way home. I hoped that the image in my head would fade by the time we got back to the house, in case I burst out laughing when I saw Leopold.

Chapter Nine

When we got back to the house, Leopold was in the process of checking the wine glasses for smudge marks. He held them up and scrutinised them one by one.

"Ah you are back, boys. Did you enjoy that walk, Matthew?"

"Yes, sir, I did. What a beautiful town this is."

Leopold smiled at me fondly.

"Where's Mama?" Wolfie asked.

"She's having a little rest before lunch. The doctor's been."

I felt itchy again thinking about leeches.

"Papa, I must play you a new tune I've just composed."

Leopold put the glass down and his face lit up with pride. "Let's go to the music room then."

Nannerl was practising the harpsichord. Wolfie sat down next to her and gave her a kiss. "Hello sister dearest, can I play Papa my new tune?"

"Do you still remember it?" I asked.

"Every note", Wolfie said, smiling. He cracked his knuckles and started to play. He played with confidence, adding little twirly bits here and there, showing off his extraordinary ability and smiling at them from time to time.

We all clapped when he finished playing.

"Bravo," Leopold cheered.

"What do you think, Papa? Should I play it on Thursday?"

Proudly, Leopold stood up and gave him a broad smile. "Yes, my son. It's very good. Shall we write it down, so the Prince Arch Bishop can read it first?"

"Very well," Wolfie said, moving to the desk in the corner of the room, where he took a quill pen and dipped it in ink. He began to throw down notes like a man possessed.

"Write it down neatly, Wolfgang," his father chided.

Wolfie finished writing down all the notes then handed the manuscript to his father, who went over it, humming the tune, accompanied by the movement of his right hand. "Well done, son, what shall you call it?"

"I am dedicating it to Matthew, as he is my friend and he was with me when I composed it," Wolfie said earnestly.

I didn't know what to say to that. I was thrilled to have met such a great composer. "Wolfie, I am honoured to be your friend. Thank you very much."

Leopold consulted his pocket watch. "I have to meet someone."

I studied Wolfie's face for a moment. "Have you got many friends? You know, people you hang out with?"

"Hang out?" Wolfie repeated, with a frown on his face.

"You know, kids your own age you do things with," I explained.

"I see. No, not really. I'm never in one place long enough to make friends."

He gave a wistful sigh, resting his head in his hands. "I've been travelling for as long as I can remember. Going from town to town, doing concerts. You meet some nice people along the way, but..." He shook his head.

I felt a pang of pity for him, for being burdened with such a great talent.

"That's until now, till I met you", he said, with a wry smile. "You're the best friend I've ever had and you have to go home in a few days' time."

"Yes, I do. I'll miss you, Wolfie." I really meant it.

"I'll miss you, too. It is a great pity you can't stay." Wolfie's china blue eyes turned liquid and he blinked hard.

"Still, there's the concert on Thursday. I'm really looking forward to watching you in action," I said brightly.

Wolfie sniffed. "Yes, that should be fun."

Sebastian came through. "Lunch is nearly ready, Master Wolfgang," he said ceremoniously. Then he bent down and whispered to Wolfie: "I think Helga has burnt the bratwurst again." He gave him a jovial wink.

"Thank you, Sebastian." Wolfie giggled. He turned towards me. "That reminds me, before you go, you must show us how to make hamburgers. I'd love to taste them."

We went to have a look in the kitchen, to see Helga. When they opened the kitchen door, a smoky smell wafted across to us. We watched Helga waving a saucepan about, trying to get the smoke out of the window. She was muttering to herself, then upon seeing us, she revealed: "Ich habe die bratwurst durchgebraten", in a deep loud voice. Her warty face was red and hot. "Never mind, Helga, that's just how I like it," Wolfie said happily, giving her a broad smile.

She hugged him and planted a big noisy kiss on his cheek. "Du bist meine liebling." (You are my sweetheart)".

Wolfie exchanged a few words with her and she nodded. "Helga says that as long as we are careful with the knives, we can help. She says there's some beef in the pantry, so we can make your hamburgers. We washed our hands first, then we put the meat through the mincer and it came out very fine. I added some salt and herbs. Could you chop up an onion finely, Wolfie? Mind and don't cut your fingers, we don't want you fainting all over the place. I'll make some breadcrumbs."

"Okidoky," he said, copying my expression.

I mixed the onion and breadcrumbs through the mince and my hands were covered in the mixture. The onion had made us both cry. I showed Wolfie how to shape the burgers. Helga hovered around, still muttering to herself. Now and again, she shook her head. When the burgers were sizzling in the frying pan (there was no grill), Helga returned. She leant her voluminous body over the pan and took a measured sniff.

"Hmmm, Schmells goot," she said, in broken English.

"Would you like to taste a bit?" I asked her, cutting a little bit off a cooked burger and handing her it on a fork. Dubiously, she put it into her mouth. Her eye twitched nervously. Then her flushed face broke into a grin. "Das ist gut, ja," she said, nodding vigorously. "Wunderbar."

When lunch was served, Wolfie and I looked at each other and giggled. Leopold ceremoniously lifted the lid off the serving dish and his eyes widened when he saw the burgers, wrapped in bread rolls, complete with lettuce and tomatoes.

"I hope this is at least edible," he said darkly.

"Such a clever boy Matteus is, he can cook," praised Wolfie's Mum.

"Thank you. Ideally, you need to cook chips with this, but there wasn't the time and the potatoes were already boiled anyway."

Nannerl helped herself to sauerkraut and prodded her burger with her fork. She smiled.

I picked the burger up with my hands and ate it. To my relief, it tasted OK. Ill at ease, Leopold cut his with his knife and used a fork to transport it to his mouth. He braced himself for the first mouthful, and looked as though he was being force-fed maggots. He chewed carefully, then his eyebrows shot up. "Mmmm. This is..." he gestured with his hand "quite delicious." Everyone agreed. Wolfie was ecstatic. He begged me to write down the recipe, so Helga and him could make them again.

"Don't forget to show us how to make these chaps you mentioned," Mrs Mozart said.

"Chaps? Oh, you mean chips," I said, with a smile.

"More wine, Matthew?" Leopold offered.

"Yes please, just a little." I was enjoying this habit of drinking wine with meals. Mum would disapprove if she found out. "You know, I shouldn't really be drinking this. Where I come from it is illegal for people under 18 to drink alcohol, at least in public."

"Really?" Mrs Mozart asked, in surprise. "Whatever for?"

"It is all right in moderation, with meals and so on. In fact, it helps the digestion," Leopold said.

"Don't you ever drink wine at home then?" Nannerl asked, lifting her glass to her lips.

"Only at Christmas time. A glass with the dinner."

"Well, fancy that," Wolfie's mother said, shaking her head.

Leopold noticed my wristwatch. "What a novel idea, wearing it around your wrist. It is much smaller than a pocket watch."

I took it off to let him have a look. "What is this button for?" Leopold asked, pressing it. The alarm went off, making him jump. He rolled his eyes, then laughed.

"That's the alarm button. It can be set to wake you up at a certain time. This button gives you the date." I pressed it for him to see.

Leopold narrowed his eyes and read the date. "(22/01/2006). Why, that's...—" he shook his head in wonder. "That's unbelievable."

"This button plays a tune," I went on, pressing it. It played the Star Trek theme tune.

"That's from my favourite programme on TV," I explained. I was met with blank stares.

Wolfie's face lit up. He said: "It's called Star Trek and it's all about space exploration. Fascinating. Matthew told me all about it. You watch it on a screen with moving pictures." Everyone laughed and wanted a shot of the watch.

"Well, young man of the future, you've really opened our eyes", Leopold said, placing a hand on my shoulder affectionately. "We shall all miss you when you have to go back."

"Will you be able to come back to visit us?" Nannerl asked. She moved her head to one side, making her curls dance up and down.

"That I don't know. It depends on Dr Gildenstein, I suppose. But I know what I want to be when I grow up: a scientist. Maybe I'll make my own time transporter and then I can come to visit you."

"Yessss. That would be wicked," Wolfie exclaimed, adopting some of my expressions. "You could pick me up and take me to your century and I could do concerts there," Wolfie enthused.

"It pleases us very much to hear that Wolfie's music will still be heard in over 200 years' time. I knew early on that he had a special talent."

"Yes, he will be the most famous composer ever. Our music teacher simply adores him. "She always says: 'Mozart was such a versatile composer, writing anything from symphonies and operas to concertos and church music. He is the unrivalled prodigy of nature'."

Wolfie went red in the face. He swallowed a lump in his throat. Tears stood in his mother's eyes. Leopold smiled warmly.

"Thank you, young man, for telling us that. It's made our lives worthwhile." Leopold said in a husky voice. "Music is his whole purpose in life."

The day of the concert had arrived. "Wolfie, shouldn't you be practising for tonight?" I asked him after our eighth game of cards.

"You sound just like Papa. He makes me practise till my fingers ache. I know the music inside out." He ticked his forehead. "It's all in here. After all, I composed it in the first place."

"You look remarkably calm. Aren't you nervous?"

"Of course not," he said happily.

There was an air of great excitement in the house that evening. Wolfie had a bath in a metal tub and came out looking pink and smelling fragrant. Leopold helped him dress. He wore his best outfit for the occasion: a sky blue jacket trimmed with gold, with matching knee breeches. White stockings and brand new buckled shoes completed the look. His head was adorned with a new wig, complete with velvet ribbon. "Wolfie, you look like a prince, my boy," said Leopold.

I had to agree. "Yes, you do look great. I wish I had brought my camera, I could have taken a picture of you."

Wolfie twirled round for our benefit. "You look good, too," Wolfie remarked. I too, had had a bath and was wearing Wolfie's newest Sunday clothes, a suit of burgundy with a white lacy shirt.

Leopold seemed a bit on edge. His twitchy fingers adjusted his neckerchief above his brown frock coat. "Shall we just run through the music again, Wolfie?"

Wolfie rolled his eyes heavenwards for my benefit. He was in a particularly silly mood, making up little rhymes, which meant nothing. Maybe it was the excitement? He certainly didn't betray any other sign of nerves. Then suddenly he started doing cartwheels around the room and miaouwing like a cat.

"Stop acting the buffoon, Wolfgang," Leopold called out edgily. "You must rest before your concert."

Chapter Ten

When we arrived at the palace gate, we were met by a selection of curious onlookers, who smiled at us and clapped their hands.

"Is that your fan club?" I asked, jokingly. I felt like a VIP myself, and very proud to be with Wolfie. Leopold led us to the portals of the grand looking entrance hall. I savoured every moment, aware of the fact that I would be back home the next day. A tall man, wearing a wig that would not look out of place on a spaniel, greeted us politely and showed us the way to go. We entered a hall full of people, dressed for the occasion. I had to stifle a giggle or two when I saw some of the ladies' towering wigs, which were decorated with all sorts of objects, including gross-looking stuffed birds. I looked at the tapestries on the wall and the ornate wall coverings. Gilded framed paintings adorned the walls. A pretty girl made eyes at me from behind a fan. I bowed to her gracefully, just like I'd seen Wolfie do. The girl smiled, showing her blackened teeth. My smile froze. I excused myself. I thought that Mr Payne, the family dentist, would make a fortune here if Dr Gildenstein transported him.

They sat down in the seats provided for special guests. Leopold and Wolfie went over to the harpsichord. Wolfie took his place and waited for the go ahead to start playing. The spaniel wig man, who still stood by the door gave him a sign, and Wolfie played a jolly march, for the Prince Arch Bishop, who slowly made his entrance.

He was dressed in long red robes with matching red skull cap. Leopold bowed to him and kissed the ring on his extended hand. He took his place on the throne at the front of the room. Everyone stood up and bowed to him. Wolfie finished playing his march, stood up and bowed to the holy man and his entourage of attendants and guests, to great applause. Then he sat down again, flicking away his coat tails with his hands. Everyone fell silent as Wolfie stretched and flexed his fingers and began to play one of his piano concertos. Joyous sounds filled the air. I glanced around and everyone was listening intently. Around the vast room stood liveried footmen, stiff as boards and with unwavering expressions on their faces. Wolfie's fingers were gliding over the harpsichord keys effortlessly. When he finished playing, people gave him a standing ovation.

I flushed with pride for the fact that Wolfie had called me his best friend. I was experiencing the magic of Mozart first hand. Nannerl played a duet with him, too. She played the harpsichord, while Wolfie played the violin. People received it with rapturous applause.

An old pockmarked man sitting next to me took out a gold snuff box and opened it, revealing a disgusting looking brown mixture. He rolled some between his fingers and lifted it to his nose, taking a measured sniff.

My eyes went to the ceiling, which was covered in ornate plastering. The opulent surroundings were a perfect foil for the quality of Wolfie's music.

After the concert, people began to disperse into the surrounding rooms.

Wolfie, Leopold and the Prince Arch Bishop were in conversation.

Nannerl returned. "I'm glad that is over. I get so nervous."

Her mother smiled and said: "You were wonderful, liebling. You both were."

I overheard two English ladies talking about their carriage trip. One of them said: "The road to Salzburg is infested with highwaymen, one has to be so careful nowadays."

"I never wear my best jewellery when I'm travelling," the other one said, waving her fan in front of her face.

Wolfie returned, eyes shining brightly. People kept stopping him to congratulate him on his music. A small group of people clapped their hands as he walked by. Wolfie bowed to them gracefully.

"That went rather well, didn't it?" he said, his face still flushed with excitement.

I'd never seen him so happy. "You were great, Wolfie. It was fantastic," I told him.

"Thank you," he said, before attending to the little group of people clamouring for his attention. I didn't get the chance to talk to him again until we left to go home. Refreshments were served in the dining room of the palace. Tables were loaded with dishes full of goodies. My eyes nearly popped out of their sockets. Each table was covered with heavy gold and green brocade tablecloths edged with golden tassels, with a beautiful centrepiece display of food and flowers. Looking at the dishes laden with various meats and fish and fancy foods I didn't recognise, people were certainly spoilt for choice. Hesitantly, I picked up a little canape.

"Those are wonderful. I've had two of them already," Nannerl said.

"What exactly is it?" I asked, holding my snack in mid air and sniffing it from a polite distance.

"Goose liver pate with cloves," she said.

I reluctantly took a bite, but was pleasantly surprised. "It tastes OK," I told her, scoffing the rest of it.

"Try a Roman chestnut in brandied sugar," Nannerl said, holding a plateful of delicious looking mounds of delicacies in front of me. They were stacked in a pyramid and reminded me of a certain TV advert. I was half expecting an ambassador with a terrible English accent to pop up from nowhere any minute now. The Roman chestnuts were delicious too, so where the pastries and the sweets.

I felt a bit queasy after all the rich foods I had tried.

On our way home after the reception, Nannerl and Wolfie started talking in backwards language. I joined in tentatively, to Nannerl's surprise and delight. We really had a good laugh. Wolfie was still buzzing with adrenaline after the concert's success.

Sebastian came into the bedroom in the evening, carrying a pile of clothes.

"Here you are Master Wolfgang," he said, putting his clothes into his drawers.

"I've laundered your friend's clothes as well."

"Thank you very much, Sebastian," I told him. He gave me a broad smile and left.

Wolfie glanced at the jeans and sighed. "What a pity that you are going home tomorrow."

We went to the shops the next day, by carriage. Nannerl had a fitting for a new dress and Wolfie's mother wanted to buy a new hat. The carriage tore through the narrow cobbled streets and my unaccustomed bottom felt decidedly sore when we reached our destination. We alighted and dispersed, agreeing to meet up again at that spot.

"Papa, can we go and buy some pastries?" Wolfie asked, gazing at the baker shop display with longing. Leopold opened his leather pouch with a drawstring and took out two coins. "Here's are five groschen each. Go and spoil yourselves." After profuse thanks we went off to spend our money. I had some coins left, and decided to take them home and show them to my parents.

When the ladies returned, laden with parcels, we left for home. We took the scenic route and I was really enjoying the journey, looking out of the window at the unspoilt beauty of the Salzburg suburbs. Then the carriage stopped abruptly, sending us and the stacked parcels flying in all directions.

Leopold scrambled upright. "What is the meaning of this, coachman?" he called out. He opened the door of the carriage and put his head out to see what was going on. He was forced back in by a nasty looking individual, who pointed a blunderbuss at him. The man said something in a course voice, but it sounded muffled, because he was wearing a black handkerchief in front of his mouth. Nannerl screamed and Mrs Mozart gasped, holding her hand in front of her mouth.

I sat rooted to the spot, not daring to move. I whispered to Wolfie. "What did he say?"

"He said: 'Your money or your life.' Shhh, just sit still and don't talk."

I imagined all sorts. We'd be killed or injured and I would miss my appointment with Dr G and never be able to return home. No more parents, no more Star Trek, no more computer games. I panicked.

Leopold sat back in his seat and a nerve began to twitch below his left eye. His mouth was set in an angry line. He seemed very calm and not frightened, just irritated. The man muttered something else and prodded him with the gun. I noticed that he was wearing a black cloak and torn black gloves. Leopold reluctantly opened his money pouch and poured the entire contents of it into the highwayman's greedy hand.

"Is that all?" he said roughly.

Leopold nodded. "I just took my family shopping." He threw his hands up in the air, in mock despair, "What do you expect, I have no money left."

The highwayman chuckled. "I understand, it's the same when I take my wife shopping." He tapped his hat, before pulling the reins on his horse and turned away. We heard the retreating steps of the horse.

Leopold sighed. "Twice in a month, I'm getting tired of this."

"So it's happened to you before?" I asked, incredulous.

"Oh, yes. Many a time. We are on the road so much with the children, touring. The secret is never to take more money than you need with you. That way, they can never fill their pockets with your hard earned cash. And another thing: never argue with them, show willing, otherwise you could pay with your life."

Now that the danger was over, I felt excited about the incident and couldn't get home to tell Neil what had happened. It was just like in the history books. When we got back we had some strudel and coffee before I had to get ready to go.

"You must come and see us again. Maybe next time you could stay a bit longer," Wolfie's Mum said.

"Yes, we could take you to Vienna for a trip." Leopold said, nodding in agreement.

Sebastian came in, wearing a puzzled frown. "This fell out of the pocket of the breeches I laundered, Master Matthew." I looked into the palm of his hand at the object, which turned out to be a £2 coin. "Thank you," I said, picking it up. I gave a wry smile, "I wish we had come across this earlier. It would have been proof enough that I came from another century." I gave it to Leopold, who was delighted with it.

Mrs Mozart gave me some Viennese souvenirs to take home to my parents and some Roman chestnuts.

"Thank you very much for having me. It's been wonderful,", I told them wholeheartedly.

Wolfie was a bit subdued.

"He is going to miss you," Nannerl said.

I changed into my own clothes and looked at my watch. "It's time to go. I've got 20 minutes to get there." I said goodbye to Wolfie's parents and left, escorted by Wolfie and Nannerl.

"Don't forget to take your violin to Herr Blomfeld to be re-strung," Leopold reminded him.

"No, papaPapa, I'll take it in to him on the way back."

We got to the Mirabell Gardens in good time. We sat on the park bench for a few minutes and chatted, before we went to the flower bed. While we had been talking, a gardener had started digging the bed over.

"Oh, no, how will we get rid of him?" I said, scratching my head.

The man bent down and picked something up. It was the coin Wolfie had put in to mark the exact spot where we had arrived, he rubbed it on his trousers and smiled, putting it in his pocket.

"Look, he's got the coin," Wolfie said.

"Never mind, as long as I'm in the middle of the flowerbed at six."

Wolfie went up to the gardener and said that there were some children running through the other flowerbeds at the other side of the gardens. The man's face clouded and he went to investigate.

"Thanks for having me, Wolfie. It's really opened my eyes. History lessons will never be the same again."

Wolfie took a sheet of paper from his jacket pocket. "Here's a copy of the music I wrote for you. You'll be able to play it yourself."

"Thank you so much, Wolfie. I will treasure it." I looked at it. On the top of the page it read: 'Dedicated to Matthew Walker, my best friend.' I felt very touched.

"It's not as though we'll be able to keep in touch, is it?" Wolfie said, with a shrug.

"No, we won't be able to send each other postcards and letters or anything."

I stepped into the circle. "Five to six."

Wolfie stepped in to say goodbye. "I'll really miss you, Matthew. You are the only real friend I've ever had," he said in a thick voice.

"Yes, I'll miss your company, too. I just wish—" I told him, feeling the threat of tears constrict my throat. I bit my lip. I felt so sorry for Wolfie. Apart from having his family, he was such a solitary boy. The only friend he had was his music.

"Better say goodbye now. Take care of yourself, Nannerl." I bowed and kissed her hand. She smiled warmly "Goodbye, Matthew. It was so nice to meet you." She wiped away a tear.

"You take care, too, Wolfie. Look after yourself. Your health is so important. Remember that."

Suddenly Wolfie lunged forward, hugging me tightly. "Goodbye, my friend," he said in a wobbly voice.

Just at that moment, Doctor Gildenstein pressed the button to transport me back to 2006. Only, I didn't arrive alone. With a zap and a whoosh, we both landed in my back garden.

Bewildered, Wolfie got up. "What happened?" he asked groggily.

I consulted my watch again. "But–... but it's not even six o'clock yet," I stammered. "Either Dr G was early or my watch is slow." I thought hard for a moment, then it came to me: "Do you remember that everyone had been fiddling with my watch at the dinner table a few days ago? It could be because of that."

"Oh," Wolfie said, glancing around him with wide eyes. "So we are—we are at your house?"

Chapter Eleven

"Welcome to the 21ˢᵗ Century, Wolfie."

"But—but—" Wolfie stammered.

"Don't worry. Dr G will soon notice what happened. He'll be checking to see if I got here all right."

"Maybe having you here will help me explain to my parents where I've been. I've got a sneaking suspicion that they won't believe me anyway."

Wolfie brushed the dust off his breeches and readjusted his knee bands. He looked very apprehensive.

"Come, let's go inside," I said. He followed me to the back door. I knocked on the door before entering. Wolfie followed closely behind me.

Mum sat at the kitchen table, staring into space. She had one hand on the telephone, as though she was willing it to ring.

"Mum, I'm home," I said.

Mum looked up with eyes as wide as saucers. "Matthew?" she whispered. "Matthew?" she said, a little louder. Then she let out a joyful shriek and jumped up. She hugged me and then smothered me with kisses. I rolled my eyes heavenwards for Wolfie's benefit.

Wolfie gave a discreet chuckle, in acknowledgement, knowing this was what mothers do.

"Mum, this is Wolfgang, my friend."

Wolfie bowed, taking her hand and kissing it respectfully. "I'm very pleased to meet you, Mrs Walker."

"What a charming boy," she said, with a giggle. "And your name – it sounds German?"

"I am from Austria," Wolfie began, but Mum, in all excitement, went into babbling mode, as mothers often do: "Come, let's go and see your father. He just got back from work. He'll be overjoyed to see you back. Oh, I am so relieved you're back. Are you hungry?"

Dad folded me into his arms and gave me a bear hug. "It's good to see you, son. We've been so worried. What happened? How did you get back? All we got was this mysterious message from a Dr Gildenstein, telling us not to worry, that you'd be home soon, but no explanation—" He stopped and his eyes were drawn to Wolfie.

"That's a long story. One that you probably won't believe," I said wistfully.

"So where do you live? Maybe you should phone your parents, young man. They're bound to be wondering where you are," he suggested kindly.

Wolfie fidgeted nervously, and looked at me for support.

"They—erm—aren't on the phone, are they Wolfie?"

"No, they aren't," Wolfie agreed, wondering what 'on the phone' meant.

"Why are you dressed like that, Wolfie? Have you been to a fancy dress party?" Mum asked, with an amused smile on her face. That was just what I had thought when I first met him.

Wolfie and I looked at each other.

"No, I always dress like this." There was a note of hurt in his voice. He was proud of his new clothes and wig.

"I see you brought your violin. Do you play?" my Dad enquired.

"Does Wolfie play the violin?" I laughed. "He's the best violinist you'll ever hear this century."

"You're having me on", Dad replied. He turned to Wolfie. "Go on, then play us a tune."

Wolfie's face lit up. He always felt confident when he was

playing music. "What shall I play?" he asked eagerly. "Only, the instrument needs re-stringing and won't sound as good."

"Give the boy a break. He must be tired and hungry," Mum said. "First things first. How about burgers and chips as a special treat?"

"Can we have some coke?" I asked hopefully, trying to make the most of Mum's sudden change of heart concerning healthy foods.

"All right, then," she agreed. She turned to the fridge, where there was a selection of coke and other usually forbidden liquids.

Wolfie stared at the fizzy liquid with interest. "What is that?" he whispered.

"It's coca cola. Nice," I took a sip. "You try it."

Wolfie took a gulp of his coke and spluttered. He put a hand to his nose.

"The bubbles—they tickle my nose," he said with a giggle.

I laughed. "Well, do you like it?"

Wolfie took another sip and nodded. "Yes, I do. It's nice. Quite unlike anything I've ever tried. How do they get the bubbles in?"

"Don't tell me that you've never tasted coke before," Dad said, with disbelief.

Wolfie looked at him and said truthfully: "No, this is the first time."

"But the boy is from Austria, that's why. Where about in Austria?" Mum asked.

"Salzburg," Wolfie said proudly.

"They must sell coke there, surely," dad said.

Uh Oh, time to change the subject, I thought. "It's a beautiful town, you should see it."

"How would you know so much about it, Matthew?" Dad asked.

"That's where we've just returned from."

"Without your passport?" Mum queried. She shifted uneasily in her seat.

"I think it's time you told us exactly what's been happening," Dad said.

I looked at my parents with their puzzled frowns.

I launched into our incredible story by starting off at the beginning. "Do you remember when I told you that I saw a face at the window in my bedroom?"

They both nodded. "Well, that was Diabolus, he's a hypnotist." Wolfie shuddered at the thought of him.

When I finished telling them, they both sat wide-eyed and open-mouthed.

"Well, son," Dad finally said, "Either you've got a good imagination or you're having us on to cover up the truth." He shook his head and an amused smile curved his lips. He pushed his glasses back on the bridge of his nose and turned to Mum. "What do you think?"

"It sounds too far fetched, I'm afraid. Come on Matthew. Tell us the real truth. What happened?"

I let out an exasperated sigh. "I told you this would happen, didn't I, Wolfie?"

He nodded his agreement. "Yes, you did."

Dad went on: So you're saying that this slip of a lad is in fact Wolfgang Amadeus Mozart?"

"Yes sir. My full name is Johannes Chrysostomus Wolfgang Theophilus Mozart." He said proudly.

Momentary confusion crossed Dad's face. He seemed taken aback. But then he said to Mum: "He could have read that in a history book."

"Play them a tune. Go on," I urged him, pointing at his violin.

"Yes, play us one of the tunes you composed," Dad thought he had him there, judging from his smug grin.

"Very well. I'll play one of my minuets," he said distractedly, having notice the piano in the corner of the room. He approached it. "You have a pianoforte," he said wonderingly. He turned to face Dad. "May I?"

"Of course," dad Dad replied.

He carefully opened the lid and studied the keys of the piano. "They've got different coloured keys than mine. It looks so—modern."

"Have a go," Dad went on.

Wolfie smiled, sat down at the instrument, wiggled his fingers and began to play his music confidently, as only he knew how to.

I watched as dadmy father's's mouth opened in wonder. When the tune was over, there was a deathly silence in the room.

"That was my minuet in F. I wrote it when I was about six, so it's a bit childish. I like the sound of your pianoforte. It's got good resonance," he said.

"Now I'll play you my first symphony, which, incidentally, I composed in this very town, a few years ago." He looked at me and hesitated, "well longer ago actually. Ach, it's so confusing, isn't it Matthew?" He frowned.

"Yes," I agreed, "Give or take 240 years." I chuckled.

He stood up, picked up his violin and started playing. Dad went to sit down. He was stunned. He watched Wolfie intently and his eyes began to fill with tears. Wolfie stopped playing and looked around the room, smiling broadly.

Dad cleared his throat and said huskily; "It's an honour to meet you, Wolfgang. You have no idea how much this means to me."

"My father's a big fan of yours, actually," I told him, "He's got a lot of your records and CD's, like I told you."

"I can't wait to hear them. It's going to be strange to hear music I haven't yet composed." He giggled.

Dad got a book off the shelf. It was a biography of Mozart, and he opened it up. He looked at a picture and then at Wolfie and smiled. "Yes, it's definitely you." He showed us a picture of a watercolour portrait of Wolfie, done when he was about nine. The likeness was extraordinary.

"Is this book about my family? Can I look at it?" Wolfie enthused.

"Well," Dad coloured slightly, realising that the book contained some things about his future that he shouldn't know about yet. "All right." So he showed him the pictures of his early life, taking care not to reveal too much.

"You play beautifully, Wolfie. Tell us all about your life and where you live."

We had a very enjoyable evening chatting. Dad was thrilled to speak to him about music and Mum loved to hear the tales about his travels in 18th century Europe.

When it was time to go to bed, I went up to have a shower.

"Make yourself at home, Wolfie. If you like to have a shower or bath, just go ahead. Matthew will show you where everything is," Mum told him.

"Thank you very much, Mrs Walker, but," he turned to face her again, with a puzzled frown. "What is a shower?"

"Come, and I'll show you how it works," she said, with a little smile, as she led him to the bathroom.

I came out, wrapped in a soft, fluffy towel, with my hair sticking up in all directions.

"You've got a nice rosy glow, Matthew," Mum said, patting me on the head. "Your turn next." Wolfie followed Mum into the bathroom gingerly. She showed him how the shower worked.

"That looks fun," he said. He looked at the toilet with interest. "Is that a water closet?"

"Yes, it is. This is how you flush it," Mum showed him. Wolfie jumped with fright when he heard the gurgling water drain away. But he became fascinated by the workings of it. He flushed it a few times just for the fun of it.

"Shall I take your wig now, Wolfie?" Mum asked, with an outstretched hand. "Don't look so worried, I'll give it back to you afterwards. You can't go into the shower with it on. It'll get ruined."

Reluctantly, he took it off and handed it to her.

"Here are some of Matthew's pyjama's. Leave your clothes on the landing. I'll put them in the washing machine."

"Thank you very much, Mrs Walker. What is a washing machine?"

"Come and I'll show you." Mum smiled. Wolfie watched in fascination, as Mum put some clothes into the machine and switched it on. "What a wonderful invention. Wait till I tell Sebastian. Is this why you have no servants, Mrs Walker? Because machines do all these things for you?"

Mum gave a chuckle. "Yes, something like that."

Wolfie slept in the spare bunk bed in Matthew's room.

"Your parents are very nice, Matthew."

"Yes, they're OK", I had to agree. "I'm glad that they believed our story in the end. My father says that we have to keep your identity a secret, though. There would be a big fuss if the story got out."

"I'll not tell anybody. I'm just your friend from Austria if anyone asks. Can I borrow some of your clothes to wear?"

"Yes, of course, let's look in my wardrobe."

In the morning, Wolfie emerged downstairs dressed in jeans, sweater ...and buckled shoes. He was also wearing his wig.

"I'll lend you a pair of my trainers. I don't think those shoes go with jeans."

"Why not?" Wolfie's lip went into a sulking mode.

"Well, let's say that you don't want to stand out in the crowd, shall we?"

I found him a pair of trainers I had recently grown out of. They were still too big for Wolfie, as he was of a slight build with small feet to match.

Wolfie took off his wig and his hair looked like it could have been the pride and joy of an Abyssinian guinea pig, sticking up in all directions. It turned out that he had washed it with conditioner, not shampoo. I put some gel in it to flatten it a bit.

"That's better. You look cool."

Wolfie looked puzzled. "I'm quite warm actually," was his reply.

"Do you want a shot of my personal stereo?"

"Your what?"

I put the headphones in Wolfie's ears and turned on the music. He looked bemused until he heard the music, which made him jump with fright as it came blaring into his unaccustomed earholes. He took the headphones off.

"What's that noise? Can you hear it, too?"

"That's garage music. It's Neil's tape. He left it behind. Don't you like it?"

"No, I don't like it at all. Haven't you got something....more pleasing to the ear?" Wolfie complained, with a face like an earwig.

"Hang on," I said, dashing into the lounge and reappearing with another CD, which I popped into the machine.

"Listen to this," I said, with a secretive smile.

"That's more like the kind of music I am used to," Wolfie said, with a satisfied nod of the head. "Who wrote it?" he asked later. "It has a familiar ring to it."

I had been watching his face for a while, bursting to tell him. "You did. Or at least, you will write that one day. Here's the CD case."

Wolfie read the words. "Eine Kleine Nachtmusik, it's really nice, isn't it?"

He flushed with pleasure and pride. "So people still listen to my music now?"

"Yes, they do. Like I told you, you will be very famous."

"If I ever get back to my century," Wolfie conceded, with a dreamy look on his face.

Wolfie was in the sitting room when the shrill sound of the telephone pierced the air. The poor boy nearly jumped out of his skin. He watched the phone for a few seconds and panicked, holding his ears.

"Can someone get that, please?" Mum called out from upstairs.

He was about to call out for help, as the wretched thing would not stop making a noise. So he touched it, slightly knocking the receiver off.

"Hello?" a voice said. "Hello? Is there anyone there?"

Intrigued, Wolfie bent down to listen to the voice coming out of the little holes in the strange contraption. He figured out that he should hold it to his ears. Gingerly, he lifted the receiver, holding it upside down.

"Matthew, is that you?" a voice asked.

Wolfie turned the receiver round. "No, it is me."

"It's WHO?"

"WHO are you?"

"Who are YOU?"

And so the conversation went until I rescued him from the strange thing that spoke to him.

"Neil?—No, you haven't got the wrong number. Oh, that is Wolfie," I said, smiling, "he's, erm, from out of town."

"It was my friend. He's coming round later."

After breakfast, I switched on the TV. From the moment I switched it on, Wolfie watched with large eyes, transfixed, like a zombie.

"It's a miracle!" he exclaimed. "This is by far the greatest invention anyone ever thought of," he said, in awe.

He kept switching channels, smiling like a maniac.

"This is wunderbar. I can't wait to tell Papa about it!"

There was one scene in a police series in which one man shot another and he lay bleeding on the ground. Wolfie screamed. "Murder! Matthew! Come quickly. That man just shot the other fellow. It's terrible. Look, he's bleeding and he's not moving." Horrified, he asked, in a low whisper: "Do you think he is dead?"

"Wolfie, don't worry, It's not real, they're just acting it. Really." I laid a hand on his trembling shoulder.

"Are you sure?" he asked in a small voice, still visibly shaken.

"Absolutely. People always die on TV. Then they pop up two days later in another show."

"Oh." His mouth formed a perfect circle and he flushed with embarrassment. "It looked so real," I heard him mutter to himself. "I saw the blood."

I changed the channel to MTV and they were playing older songs. The video of the song 'Money' by Jamelia came on.

"Yes, I like this. But I don't understand, they are wearing clothes from my century."

I smiled to myself. I watched Wolfie with amusement as he discovered rock, pop, soul, jazz and punk all in one morning. He was fascinated at all the different styles of music we have. "They have such freedom to compose what they like, it's incredible," he enthused. "I don't think the Prince Archbishop would agree with it, though."

Later on, we went for a walk. Poor Wolfie nearly died of fright when he saw cars for the very first time. He clung to me, trembling, and muttered: "What are those?"

"They're cars. Don't worry, they won't bite. This is how we get about. It's much faster than a horse drawn carriage, much less bumpy and far more comfortable, I'd say." Wolfie looked shocked and pale, sticking close by me all the way home. He didn't say another word until we got back into the house.

Neil came round after lunch. I introduced him to Wolfie, but followed Dad's advice about not telling him or anyone about his identity. "Pleased to meet you, Nike," Wolfie said, reading the word on Neil's T-shirt.

"My name is Neil, not Nike."

"Oh, I beg your pardon, but I thought that—" his voice tailed off, pointing at his T-shirt. He would have to get used to this modern habit of people wearing words on their clothing.

Neil was no sooner in the house than he let out a torrent of questions about my disappearance. "Where have you been? Who kidnapped you? When did you get back? How did you get back?" were some of the questions he fired at me.

"Hold on a minute," I said, holding up my hand. "Too many questions."

I answered most of them truthfully, also about having been to Salzburg, only not that I had visited it in another century.

We played some computer games. Then we visited the website of the caves of Diabolus, but there was no-one there, not a soul in the caves, so poor Wolfie worried about Dr G, and Spike and where they were, and whether he would ever be able to return home now.

"Do you want to go for a run in the car?" Dad suggested.

Wolfie's face registered fear. "I don't know, is it safe?"

"Don't worry, Wolfie, you'll enjoy it," I told him.

"Very well," he said reluctantly.

We got into the car and Dad started up the engine. Wolfie sat rigid with fear. His lips moved silently.

"What are you doing?" I asked.

"I'm praying."

When we took off he put his hands over his eyes.

"Are you all right, Wolfie?" Dad asked.

"Yes, thank you." Wolfie peeped through his fingers. When he saw a bus approach, he hid his eyes again.

"There's nothing to worry about, Wolfie, Wolfie. Just relax." I patted his shoulder.

It took several minutes for him to relax and eventually he did take his hands away from his face and watched the passing traffic.

"Where are we going, Dad?"

"Aha," he went, tapping his nose. We were driving through Chelsea. After a while, he said: "I thought Wolfie might like to see where he used to live." He pulled into a parking space and we walked from then on. We turned into Ebury Street.

Wolfie was excited. "There it is, on the other side of the street. I recognise the house." Wolfie observed the still familiar surroundings. The house, typical of its age, had tall windows and the bottom part of the outside wall was painted in a warm shade of cream, the top part was left in the old dark red brickwork.

Wolfie touched the iron gate. "I used to swing from this. Papa always told me off for doing it." He smiled. "The house hasn't changed a bit." His eye caught the commemorative plaque on the wall of the house. "Oh, look. There is my name."

"It also says that you wrote your first symphony here, is that true?"

"Yes, it is. Oh, wait till I tell Papa that I stood on this very spot."

"Oh and look, the little stone bench is still there, too. I used to sit on it."

"I've brought my camera. Let's take a photograph, then you can show it to your family."

"How interesting. How does that contraption work, Matthew?"

I looked at dad, who was happy to give Wolfie a detailed explanation.

We took a few photos of Wolfie in front of the house, one of

Wolfie and I together and then dad Dad said:
"I've got another surprise for you. Come." We followed him across the street and into a square. There, in the middle of the square stood a statue.

"Go on, go and have a look at it," Dad urged, with a smile.

Wolfie and I went up closer. It was a statue of Wolfie holding a violin, aged about nine, the time that he lived in London. Wolfie was delighted.

"A statue of me. What an honour!" he exclaimed. He felt elated. We took more photos before we left. Wolfie went into a kind of hyperactive overdrive, because of all the excitement. Either that or he'd drunk too much coke. He was tapping his hands on his handrest, his feet were tapping out a rhythm and his mouth never stopped either. I'd never seen him like that and he was giving me a headache.

As we drove through London, Wolfie remarked: "I can't believe how many buildings have been built since I lived here. When I lived in Chelsea, this was all countryside, it's remarkable."

Wolfie recognised a lot of the buildings, especially Buckingham Palace, which he called Buckingham House, as it was known in his era, when he had performed in front of King George III and was presented with fifty ducats.

"I wonder if you'll remember the next place we'll visit," Dad said. As soon as the building came into view, Wolfie smiled.

"The British Museum and Library," he said knowingly. "I presented them with a manuscript when I was nine. It was called 'God is Our Refuge and our Strength', a motet I wrote."

"Do you want to see if it's still here?" Dad asked.

"Yes, please. It was the first piece I set in English," he explained.

"Yes, and the only one, I'm afraid," Dad said.

We walked through the vast library section. We asked for assistance and a museum orderly showed us the Mozart collection, which contained various memorabilia, including Wolfie's motet, which was now a yellowing manuscript.

"Imagine that, they've still got it," he said softly, with a giggle. "Just look at the writing. So untidy, and I had to bend the bars to get all the notes in. Dreadful."

"Can I please take a closer look at it?" he asked the museum orderly.

"I'm afraid that is out of the question, young man. It is a very valuable document and no-one is allowed to handle it."

"Fancy that." He smothered another giggle.

The museum orderly gave him a curious look.

"There is a lock of hair," I noticed, pointing at the neatly tied blond lock, which was behind glass and framed in a gilt frame.

"A lock of my hair?" he whispered to me. "Now how did they get that?" He touched his hair nervously.

The sharp eared orderly was beginning to look at us suspiciously, so Dad said: "Come on, you two, it's time to leave," I cast a backward glance and noticed him still staring at us as we left the building.

We went to McDonald's for tea. Wolfie wolfed down his quarter pounder with great gusto. "This is delicious, I wish we had one of these eateries in Salzburg. You are so lucky, Matthew."

He took another gulp of coke. He had that dreamy look again. "Mr Walker, would it be all right for me to buy some music paper? I have a tune in my head I simply have to get down on paper." He rummaged in his pocket for money and unearthed some Austrian money of his time.

My Dad just smiled. "Put your money away, Wolfie. You won't get very far with it here. Come, I know where we can buy some."

Wolfie spent the rest of the day throwing notes down on paper like a boy possessed. Then later on, he played it for us. It was fantastic. Dad's eyes welled up when he heard it. He gulped hard and said: "Wolfie, you simply have no idea what an honour it is to have you staying with us."

Beaming with pleasure, he took a bow and said: "The honour is all mine."

Dad and Wolfie spent hours discussing musical strategies and, although I really liked him playing his music, it was all a bit above my head, so I left them to their conversations.

Wolfgang could hold a good reasoned discussion with adults and he was surprisingly bright for his age.

Dad also discussed his inventions with Wolfie, who was fascinated and listened attentively.

Chapter Twelve

The days went by and there was still no sign of Dr G, so Wolfie became quite anxious.

It was decided that he should come to school with me on Monday morning. He seemed quite keen. He was being home taught by his father, like lots of children in his era, so it would be even more of a novelty for him to go to a proper school.

"Now remember, Wolfie: You're supposed to be from this century. You're my friend from Austria and you're visiting us."

"I won't forget. I AM your friend and I AM from Austria on a visit here, so that's all true," he said, with a little shrug.

"Yes, as long as you don't tell anybody you're from 1767 or how you got here, OK?"

"OK." He nodded.

"And please take your wig off. You look a bit odd in school uniform with a wig on. It just doesn't go together."

Wolfie sighed. "Very well." He took it off with a sulky pout and ruffled his own hair.

"If you ask me, you 21st century people don't care much about your appearance," he grumbled.

We walked to school and when we reached the school gate, Wolfie stopped in his tracks. "Are you sure that you want me to come? What if they find out who I am?"

Wolfie stopped in his tracks and stared open-mouthed at a group of girls walking by. He couldn't believe his eyes. "Massew, those girls, they are showing their knees. Their—erm—garments are so short, is that allowed here?"

I chuckled. "Yes, it's allowed. Women have been wearing short skirts for years. It's just as well you didn't arrive here in the sixties, you would probably have fainted."

"And their hair—it's undressed," he said, his voice a mixture of reproach and wonder.

Just then, one of the girls from my class walked by and kissed me on the cheek. "We've all missed you, Matthew. Glad you are back."

Wolfie's cheeks turned pink. He couldn't imagine a girl kissing his cheek.

The school bell went.

"Close your mouth, Wolfie. You'll catch flies," I said to him, playfully hitting him on the head with a ruler.

In a daze, he followed me into the school building. He looked around the large classroom with curious eyes.

"You can sit here," I told him, pointing at the space beside me. "Neil won't mind." All my friends were pleased to see me back and we all chatted animatedly, as I introduced them to Wolfie.

"Watch it, there's old camel face," Neil whispered, as Miss Jennings appeared. She clapped her hands. "Less noise, please. I know you're all excited to see Matthew back, but we have to get on with our lessons." The class fell silent. She came over to meet Wolfie. "So this is your friend from Austria. I hope you'll enjoy your stay here, Wolfgang Pertl."

Wolfie had chosen his mother's maiden name for anonymity.

Enchanted, he got up and was about to bow and kiss her hand, I had to give him a swift prod in the side to remind him not to. Instead he nodded. "Thank you, Miss Jennings."

"Maybe you could give us a little talk about life in Austria sometime? I'm sure everyone would like to find out more about you and what life is like over there?"

92

Wolfie gave me a stricken look, then faced her, saying:
"I – erm—"

"My friend is very shy, Miss Jennings," I said, springing to his defence.

Her neck swivelled round and she faced me. "Very well, when he settles in a bit, he'll feel more up to it. Better still, everyone can write down questions for him to answer. That won't be so bad, will it, Wolfgang?"

Wolfie said "No, Miss Jennings."

"I tried to get you out of that one," I whispered to him. We did maths, at which Wolfie was brilliant.

"I didn't know you were so brainy, Wolfie," I said, looking at him in admiration.

"I love mathematics, beside music, it's my favourite subject."

I knew that, as a result of all his travels, Wolfie could speak French, Latin and Italian, as well as English and German, his own language.

At break time, we went out to the playground and we were surrounded by all my classmates, wanting to find out what had happened. I had to choose my words carefully, in case they found out about Wolfie's real identity.

Wolfie enjoyed his first day at school. He enjoyed feeling part of a group. He sat down on one of the benches in the playground and opened up his bag of crisps and drank his carton of orange juice and watched me in conversation.

"Hi, Wolfgang. My name is Lucy." A pretty dark-haired girl with soft brown eyes sat next to him on the bench. Wolfie stopped himself from bowing to her and kissing her hand.

"Enchanted to meet you, Lucy," he said, trying to keep his eyes from straying to her bare knees.

"You are really good at Maths, aren't you?"

"Not bad, I suppose," he admitted, giving an awkward little shrug.

"I've been to Austria, you now. Skiing with my parents. It's a lovely country."

"Where in Austria did you go?" Wolfie asked politely.

"Kitzbuhl. It's lovely there." She took a crisp from her packet. "Do you want one of these?" she asked, thrusting the packet at him.

"What are they?" he asked, eyeing up the strangely shaped crisps.

"Monster Munch, they're really good."

Wolfie's face froze into a forced smile. "No thank you, I—would you like some of mine?"

She took one out of his packet. "Thanks." She smiled at him, then sighed. "History next. It's so boring." She pulled a face.

"I am rather looking forward to it," Wolfie said.

The bell went and they all trouped inside again.

"See that girl over there?" Wolfie said, with a discreet nod in her direction.

I looked. "Lucy?"

"Yes, that's her name, do you know that she was eating monster meat at break time?" Wolfie pulled a disgusted face.

I laughed. "Do you think—hahaha—No, Wolfie, it's Monster Munch, not really anything to do with monsters. It's just a flavour, silly."

"Oh" he said, colouring slightly. "I feel foolish now."

In class, Miss Jennings said: "Now, Matthew, I don't suppose you've started with your history project yet, as you were—erm—absent for so long.

"No, Miss Jennings, but I know which era I'd like to do," I told her with enthusiasm.

"Oh?" Her eyebrows shot up in surprise. "Tell me."

"18ᵗʰ Century Austria", I said, with a smile. After all, I'd actually spent some time there, not that I could reveal that.

"Well, that's very interesting, Matthew. Good luck with it." She gave an approving nod, but looked a bit puzzled at my change of attitude about the subject.

She faced Wolfie. "I suppose you'll be able to help Matthew with it, since you're Austrian and have probably covered the subject at your school."

"Yes, I'd like to help him."

"Good, good," she said. She walked back to the blackboard. "Today, we are going to cover the subject of Victorian Britain." Wolfie's eyebrows shot up questioningly. He looked at me and grimaced.

"19th Century, I'm afraid," I explained.

"Oh, let's hope that I don't get asked any questions. Luckily he wasn't, but he listened with great interest to everything that Miss Jennings had to say. For him, all this was the future, not the past.

The lunchtime bell went. Lucy went to sit beside Wolfie in the dining room.

"I think you've got a really nice accent, Wolfie," she told him.

"Thank you, Lucy", he replied, blushing a little.

Neil and I burst into giggles and whispered to each other.

"What are you two sniggering about?" Lucy asked.

"You fancy him, don't you?" Neil said.

It was Lucy's turn to blush this time. Wolfie looked at his plate.

"So? Is there a law against it?" she said huffily. She pushed a strand of her shoulder length brown hair behind her ear and whispered to Wolfie: "Don't take any notice of them. They're just being childish. How old are you by the way?"

"I'll be 11 tomorrow," Wolfie said, with a smile on his face.

"It's your birthday tomorrow?" Lucy shrieked.

"Yes, it is actually," he admitted shyly.

"Did you know this, boys? It's Wolfie's birthday tomorrow."

"Course we knew," I told her, with a wink.

"That's brill," Lucy responded, getting the message.

Later on, when Wolfie was out of earshot, I asked her and a few others to come over to my house the next day, so that we could give him a surprise party.

When we got home that afternoon, we went into the kitchen for a drink. Mum said: "I made you a nice beef casserole in the slow-cooker this morning. It's nearly ready." She wiped her hands on her apron.

Wolfie eyed the slow cooker with interest. "How does it cook if you don't put it on the stove?"

"It's electric, Wolfie, you plug it in. See?" She demonstrated it to him.

"Oh, yes, I see." He sounded unconvinced. "But how come—"

While Mum and I chatted he had a closer look, then let out a bloodcurdling scream.

"What happened?" Mum called out, worried.

With a trembling hand he pointed at the plughole.

"That thing bit me," he said, shaken.

"You're as white as a ghost, lad. Here, take a drink of water," Mum said, sitting him down in the lounge.

"Thank you," he said weakly.

"You've had an electric shock. You must be careful, Wolfie. Electricity is very dangerous." She sounded concerned.

I put on the TV to take his mind off it. Within seconds, his eyes were glued to the set. We watched various children's programmes and when Blue Peter came on, he asked: "Which one's Peter?"

"Erm, I don't think any of them are called Peter."

He threw me a quick glance. "One of them must be called Peter, why else would they call the programme Blue Peter?" He snorted. "Is he blue?" he muttered.

Mum and I exchanged bemused glances, trying to keep a straight face.

"You do have a point, Wolfie," I said.

We watched Neighbours, during which Wolfie's jaw dropped. They were doing a beach scene, during which the actors wore swimming gear.

Going red in the face, he whispered: "She's virtually naked. What would her father say if he saw her like that?" He tutted, shielding his eyes, but he peered through his fingers all the same.

"Yes, you may well ask," Mum said, with a smile in her voice.

I wondered what he would do on Monday, when we had swimming at school.

"Do you want to watch another Star Trek episode? I've got lots on video.

"All right then."

Wolfie became so engrossed in Star Trek that he had to be told three times that dinner was ready. "We can watch the rest afterwards," I assured him.

"If you lived in this century permanently, I doubt if you'd get much composing done, Wolfie," Dad said, with a chuckle.

He went to put on a CD. Wolfie recognised it at once. "My first symphony. Imagine that." He ate his food with relish, complimenting Mum on the lovely dinner, and when it came to dessert, he took a small helping of fruit salad.

"Try some ice cream," I offered. "It's really nice."

"Yes, please," he watched me spoon it over his fruit. Then he took a mouthful and nearly hit the roof. "Oh, that's cold," he said, with a shiver. He held his cheek "It hurts."

"You must have sensitive teeth, Wolfie. Maybe you need to see the dentist."

"The dentist?" he asked dubiously.

He took another, smaller mouthful. "It's all right on the other side of my mouth, it doesn't hurt there. This is really delicious."

After dinner, we watched the rest of the Star Trek video. Wolfie thought it fascinating. "It's a bit like what we've been through, isn't it? You know: Beam me up, Doctor Gildenstein," he observed.

"Yes, I suppose you're right," I agreed.

"I wish I could go into space. Just imagine—" He went on dreamily.

"Can we play a game on your computer now?"

The next morning, Wolfie rose early. He was still excited at discovering things in a different century, just like I had been in Salzburg. He had a look around the kitchen. He opened and shut the fridge a few times, feeling the cold air with his hand and wondering how it was possible to keep it so cold in there. He opened the freezer, too and touched the shelves. He withdrew his hand rapidly, "That's really cold." He looked at the kettle for a moment and followed the lead with his eyes to the plug in the wall. He was baffled with this thing called electricity, which seemed to make everything work in the home.

"Are you hungry, Wolfie?" Mum stood in the doorway, all dressed and ready for work. She filled op the kettle and switched it on.

"Hello, Mrs Walker, I was just looking at all these machines. How wonderful it must be to be able to just press a button and make things work. My mother wouldn't believe me if I told her."

"It does make life easier, I suppose, and it leaves you much more time to do other things. That's why most women work nowadays. The only thing is, you take it all for granted. You realise this when there is a power cut and nothing works for a while." She poured the water over the tea-leaves in the tea pot.

Wolfie watched, with interest. "Don't you lock your tea away, Mrs Walker? It's so expensive. My mother's got a special little chest for it with a lock."

"Really?" Her eyebrows shot up. "It's not expensive nowadays, maybe it is where you come from, but not here."

"My mother sometimes has tea parties when all her friends come round and drink tea," Wolfie went on, watching her stir the tea round in the pot.

"Would you like a cup?"

"Oh, can I? Please?" He sounded excited. "Are you sure?"

She smiled. "Of course. It's probably better for you than all that Coke you've been drinking." She poured him a cup and he sat at the kitchen table savouring every drop of it.

"By the way: "Happy birthday, Wolfie."

He flushed with pleasure. "Thank you."

Wolfie went outside to listen to the birds singing, a habit he always enjoyed.

Later, at the breakfast table, I handed Wolfie his present and card. "A present for you."

Wolfie's eyes widened. "Thank you, it is lovely," he said, admiring the wrapping paper with all its pretty colours.

"Open it, then," I urged him.

Carefully, so as not to tear the paper, he opened it, and gasped as he saw the box. "It's one of those music boxes. Thank you so much, Massew."

"It's called a personal stereo," I explained.

His eyes filled with tears. "I don't know what to say—it's wonderful."

Dad coughed discreetly. "Here's something to put in it. A selection of my CDs."

"But, sir, you'll miss them," Wolfie said hesitantly.

"Don't worry, I can get some more."

Wolfie looked at them. There were at least three early Mozart and three Beethoven CDs, plus a selection of other popular classics.

"You can let your father hear the Beethoven music," he told Wolfie.

"I would love to meet this Beethoven fellow, he's really good."

"Ah, but you will meet him one day. He'll come to see you in Vienna when he's about 17. You'll be teaching him composition."

His face lit up. "Really? How fascinating."

"Here's something from me", Mum said, handing him another parcel. It was a shoebox full of batteries, which would keep the personal stereo going for a long time.

"Thank you all so very much. You've been wonderful to me."

"Here," Mum handed him a tissue. He blew his nose loudly and sniffed.

Chapter Thirteen

Mum told me to go to granny's house after school, so that all the surprise party guests had a chance to arrive before us. We had an enjoyable time there. Apart from when Wolfie visited the toilet and we heard him scream. He had taken fright at a pair of false teeth in a glass in the bathroom.

When we got back home, the front door was decorated with balloons.

"How lovely, what are they?" Wolfie asked.

"They're balloons. You blow them full of air and then you burst them," I explained. I picked one up from the floor in the hallway and demonstrated it.

Wolfie jumped with fright.

"Matthew, stop being mean," Mum called out. She laid a consoling hand on Wolfie's shoulder. "You put up balloons when you celebrate someone's birthday."

"How novel. Can I hold one?" he asked tentatively.

They went into the sitting room. It was full of school friends.

"Surprise!" they all shouted merrily.

Wolfie gazed around the room in a dream-like state.

He was very moved. "Thank you so much, what a lovely thing to do." He went over to kiss Mum's cheek and shook Dad's hand. He looked so earnest and there were tears in his eyes.

His eyes widened when he saw the table laden with food: sandwiches, quiches, pizza, sausage rolls, crisps and snacks, cakes and biscuits. I was secretly relieved that Mum had produced conventional foods kids like, and not a display of obscure health foods that usually graced our table.

"It's a veritable feast," Wolfie exclaimed, grinning from ear to ear.

"Now for the piece de resistance: your birthday cake." Mum proudly brought it in and put it in the space reserved for it on the middle of the table.

"It's shaped like a violin", he said, clapping his hands together. "Oh, how wonderful, Mrs Walker."

"I made it myself. I hope you like it," she said, with a beaming face, happy to see him so thrilled."

"But it is too lovely to eat," he said.

"Let's take a photo of it. Then you'll be able to look at it again, when you get home," Dad said. He took out his camera and took a photo of the cake, one of Wolfie and me and of everyone enjoying themselves. Wolfie got a bit of a shock when the flashbulb went, he though that lightning had struck.

"Yes, mother, I must say that this cake is one of your best efforts yet," I said, with a grin. "Remember when you made a cake for my cousin Emma. The one that was supposed to be a ballerina?"

Mum laughed. "Yes, unfortunately she ended up looking like an ugly sister, with shoulders that would make a boxer proud." She held up her hand. "Don't remind me."

Wolfie had a wonderful time opening presents and cards. Lucy gave him a Star Trek book, with which he was very pleased. "How did you know I liked Star Trek?" he asked her.

She flushed with pleasure. "I asked Matthew what you would like."

"Well, I am really happy with it, thank you very much". He took her hand and wanted to kiss it, but at the last moment he changed his mind and kissed her cheek instead.

"Wolfie," I chided, with a mock serious face.

"Well, she's not wearing any rouge, is she," he retorted, with a little smile.

Lucy was delighted at the attention she was getting.

Wolfie also got a 'Hits 2006' CD from Neil and a pencil case, a book, sweets and other things from the others.

"You're doing all right today, aren't you, Wolfie," I said.

"It's the best birthday party I have ever had."

They ate and drank fizzy drinks and coke and when it was time to cut the birthday cake, they urged him to blow out the candles, singing 'Happy Birthday' to him.

"You have to make a wish, but not tell anyone what you wish for, or else it won't come true," Lucy informed him.

Wolfie blew out all of his eleven candles and closed his eyes to make a wish.

We all clapped and cheered. I put on some music and some of the kids were dancing, disco style. Wolfie watched with interest and tried to follow some of the moves they made. I sat down beside him.

"Not quite the dancing style you're used to, I'd say."

"No, but it looks fun. I'm willing to learn," he said, tapping his foot in time to a Robbie Williams tune.

"Well, come on then, what are you waiting for?" I dragged him to his feet and jokingly 'pushed' him in with the rest of the dancers. At first he looked a bit stiff and unsure of himself, but once he got going, he danced very well. He was light on his feet and had the natural feel of the music.

He glanced at Lucy, who gave him a broad smile. He went over to her and pulled her into the dancing crowd. The music had changed to Kylie Minogue. "I was told that you are a very good musician, is that true?" Lucy asked him. "Yes, I am actually," he replied, then saw her startled expression. She was obviously taken aback at his frankness and his lack of modesty.

Hastily, he added: "I don't want to sound conceited, but yes, I am good. I've been playing music for most of my life and I've been giving concerts since I was six."

"Will you play something for us later?" she asked, looking at him appealingly. "Oh, I don't know," he said, with a hesitant shrug. "Go on, for me," she wheedled, looking into his eyes.

"All right then, my dear Lucy, I shall serenade you," he kissed her hand. "But first, let's dance some more."

Lucy kept him to his word. When there was a quieter moment, she said: "Wolfie's going to play some music now."

"Yes, that's a great idea," I agreed. All the kids sat down and looked at him expectantly when he took the violin and started to play part of a violin concerto. I observed Lucy as she watched him play. The girl was clearly smitten with him. She gazed at him adoringly. When he stopped playing, they all clapped. I went to pat him on the back. "Great, isn't he? He plays the piano, too." Wolfie was in seventh heaven, he loved being in the centre of attention when it came to music. He played a variety of tunes for them.

"Don't you need sheet music?" someone piped up.

He chuckled. "No, I play from memory."

"You're not even looking at the keys," Neil said.

"He can play blindfolded. Can't you, Wolfie?" I put in.

Wolfie nodded cheerfully.

"Go on, show us," Sam called out. "Yes, let's blindfold him then," Neil said.

"All right," Wolfie said, with a gleam on his face. Sam tied a scarf around his head. He continued to play, just as good, to everyone's delight.

Dad produced some sheet music, mostly Sixties and Seventies stuff, like the Beatles and Abba.

We all sang along to 'Yellow Submarine' and 'Money Money Money'

"This has been a fantastic party," Lucy declared.

"Yes, it has," Wolfie agreed. "Thank you again for the lovely present, I shall treasure it always."

Lucy chuckled. "It's only a book."

"Every time I read it I will think of you", he went on. "I shall remember your lovely face and your gentle smile. You will be the inspiration for my music. I shall dedicate a sonata to you."

"Oh, Wolfie," Lucy breathed, her cheeks turning pink, "You've got a lovely way with words." She left, walking on air.

Neil, who had overheard the exchange, made a 'pretend to make yourself sick by sticking your fingers down your throat'—gesture with his fingers.

"That is like, so gross," he exclaimed. "When do you two get married?"

Wolfie coloured slightly. "We are just good friends. She is a charming girl. Don't you have any girlfriends?"

Neil made a mock-horrified face. "Yuk, definitely not. You are so sad."

"Quite the contrary, dear fellow, I am very happy."

After everyone left, Neil, Wolfie and I helped clear up. When Mum took out the vacuum cleaner and switched it on. Intrigued, Wolfie watched, as she walked up and down with it.

"Please may I have a go?" he asked her.

"With pleasure, here you are. You just walk up and down with it and it sucks up dirt and dust." Wolfie was thrilled and enjoyed his task immensely.

"Thank you Wolfie, you are doing a great job."

"I had a wonderful time today, Matthew. I'm so glad that I got zoomed back with you. I'll have so much to tell my parents and Nannerl now."

We had cookery at school the next morning. Mrs Parker, the cookery teacher showed us how to make pancakes. She was an expert at tossing them into the air to turn them over in the pan. When she did it, she always caught them. We all had a go at it and when Wolfie tossed his pancake, it landed on the ceiling and refused to come down again. Everyone thought this was so funny, seeing the pancake stubbornly stuck to the ceiling. Wolfie in particular. He started laughing. His infectious hyena giggle made everyone laugh, too. Soon, the whole classroom was bursting with laughter, bringing forth Miss Jennings, who stepped into the cookery class, looking as though she'd been sucking lemons.

"What on earth is going on!" she called out, casting a quick glance around the room to seek the culprit of the laughter outburst. Everyone stopped and there was the occasional snort or giggle. Apart from Wolfie, who just couldn't stop laughing. When all the others had fallen silent, he was still at it. I poked him in the ribs.

Miss Jennings marched up to him. His laughter died down eventually. She stood before him, nostrils flared like an ostrich, right underneath the stranded pancake.

"What is the meaning of this? Wolfgang, I am very disappointed in you. Such behaviour is only permitted in the Zoo," she said sternly.

Wolfie tried hard to stop the next giggle, but there it was. He put his hand in front of his mouth to stop himself. He went red in the face. She directed her gaze at me. "I thought you said that your friend was shy, Matthew. It appears not to be the case. Therefore," she faced Wolfie again, "You can do your little talk about Austria after break time." As she turned to walk away, the stranded pancake decided to dislodge itself and promptly fell on top of her head. It made her look utterly foolish. The whole class burst out laughing again. Even Mrs Parker had problems stifling a giggle.

Miss Jennings took the offending pancake off her head and looked at the ceiling, which now bore a greasy mark. "Hmmm," she went, lost for words. Jaws clenched, fuming with anger, she walked out of the classroom, without looking back.

Wolfie was declared the hero of the day, for embarrassing Miss Jennings. During break time, he walked around with his personal stereo, munching a bag of crisps. He was so engrossed in his Wagner CD, that he forgot to take it off when he went back into the classroom. He sat down at his desk, his mind clearly elsewhere, and he tapped the rhythm of the music on his desk. At one point, he started humming the tune, not realising that he was doing it. The class was silent, apart from Wolfie, who sat, with his eyes closed, making percussion noises with his hands and humming along to the music.

Miss Jennings' eyes narrowed and her mouth was set in a grim line. She took four great strides and then she stood before Wolfie.

She took the headset from his stereo off, she said "Boo" into his ear.

Wolfie got such a fright that he jumped up and gasped. He stared into Miss Jennings' face in horror.

"Wolfgang Pertl, I've just about had enough of you."

"Oh, I'm sorry, Miss. I forgot that I still had this on, I—" he uttered, going red in the face.

"Yes, it appears so, doesn't. Your generation seems to have been born with these things welded to your ears. It's a disgrace." Her voice rose in anger. "Why do you listen to this rubbish...this... monotonous claptrap is beyond me. You children don't know what good music is. Whatever happened to Bach, Beethoven and Mozart's music?" She took the CD out of Wolfie's personal stereo.

"In my time—This noise they now call music was not around. All this disco rubbish, and Britney whatsername, and—" She put on her glasses and took a look at the label on the CD. "Wagner?" she said, the surprise in her voice gave way to her anger subsiding. "You're listening to Wagner, Wolfie?" She suddenly realised that she looked foolish and handed him back his CD. "Well, I've got nothing against that sort of music, only not during class, all right, Wolfgang?"

"No, Miss Jennings."

She glanced at him over her glasses. "Do you like Wagner, Wolfgang?" Her tone of voice softened. "Isn't it a bit, well— advanced for you?" she asked.

Wolfie thought for a moment. "Well," he began, "I find his music richly expressive and intensely illustrative. Especially sections of 'Lohengrin' and 'Wotan's Farewell' I find moving."

Miss Jennings was lost for words for the second time that day. "Yes," she said inadequately, baffled with this strange boy, who had come to join them.

"Wolfie takes his music very seriously," Lucy explained.

"So I gather," she said. "Well," she clapped her hands together and straightened herself. "Let's get on with some work then. Wolfie is going to answer some questions about Austria now."

"Am I?" he said, looking worried.

In a whisper, I warned him: "Don't mention the Emperor, don't let on that you've never been to school and for God's sake don't mention that you don't have electricity in Austria."

One of the boys put up his hand.

"Yes, Charlie, you may ask him a question," Miss Jennings said, with a nod of the head.

"How come you speak English so well, Wolfie? Did you learn it at school?"

"Well, my father taught me and I have lived in London for a while when I was younger."

"Is your father a teacher?"

"No, but he is very learned and knows a lot of things. My father is a violinist and Kapellmeister for the Prince Archbishop." There, it had slipped out before he could help himself. He looked at me and grimaced. Miss Jennings looked puzzled for a moment, but her expression settled to one of interest.

"Did your father teach you how to play the piano and violin?" she asked.

"Yes, he did, Miss."

Someone asked him what he liked best about England. He found it a hard question to answer. He wanted to say that he liked the way everything worked with pressing buttons and switches. That he loved watching TV and playing with the computer but of course he was aware that he couldn't mention that.

"Well, I really like the people, they are so friendly. I like the school, and I like staying at Matthew's house and I love the ice cream."

"Right, one more question, please," Miss Jennings said, pointing at a boy with a shock of fuzzy black hair in dire need of a comb.

"How do you feel about the fact that Hitler came from your country?" a boy called Thomas asked.

Wolfie frowned. "Hitler?" He shook his head. "I don't know of him. Was he a composer?"

There were gasps all round. The class had just covered World War II and Hitler in a project. "Oh, no," I said under my breath and hid my face behind my hand.

Miss Jennings said: "Come on, Wolfgang. Stop being silly. Hitler, as you well know, was not a composer."

Wolfie looked at her helplessly and shook his head.

"But, Miss, I have never heard of him, honestly."

"I find that very hard to believe, young man. Don't they teach you history at school? Or have you just got your head in the clouds listening to music all the time," she chided gently.

She suddenly felt sorry for Wolfie and cast a glance at the boy who asked the question. "Not a very tactful thing to ask, is it now, Thomas?"

"But who was this man Hitler then? I'd like to know," Wolfie asked, in a little voice.

Thomas stood up and said: "Hitler caused World War II. He made millions of people die."

"World War Two?" Wolfie frowned again, looking over at me with a stricken look. "I'm very sorry about that. I never knew." His expression fell and he was visibly upset that someone from his beloved country could have done such a thing. He felt ashamed.

Luckily they went onto another subject, to Wolfie's relief.

Lucy approached him afterwards. "I'm sorry about that Hitler-business. Thomas should never have brought that subject up," she said, linking her arm through his.

"That's all right. I really have never heard of him." He looked her square in the face and said: "You must think I'm really stupid not knowing about Hitler and the war." He sighed. "I wish I could tell you the real reason that I don't know these things, but I can't."

"Wolfie, I think you are the cleverest boy I've ever met. You're a very talented musician, you're brilliant at maths and you can speak other languages fluently. I think you are wonderful."

Wolfie looked at her as though he was seeing her for the first time. Then he put his hand on her cheek and said: "And you, Lucy, are the kindest, gentlest, and the most beautiful girl I've ever met."

Chapter Fourteen

Wolfie dreaded the swimming session that followed. I had lent him a pair of swimming shorts and he felt so self-conscious wearing them that he didn't want to leave the changing rooms. He pulled the hems down to try and make them longer so that they would cover more of his white legs. He looked at his thin body in the mirror and felt so embarrassed at having to go out there half naked. His father would surely have called it indecent exposure of too much flesh.

"Wolfie, are you ready?" I called out, standing there ready in my blue swimming shorts and goggles on. I looked into his changing cubicle.

"I can't go like this. Lucy will see me and laugh," he whined.

"Nobody will look at you. You look fine anyway, come on."

"And I can't swim anyway." He pulled on his T-shirt to cover up his lily white chest.

"Oh, I give up," I said, in mock-seriousness.

People did look at him, but only because he was wearing a T-shirt.

"What is that strange smell?" Wolfie asked, twitching his nose as we approached the pool.

"That's chlorine, to disinfect the water," I explained.

"What does that mean?"

"It kills germs."

"What are germs?" He peered into the water looking for creatures called germs.

"Wolfie, are you coming in?" Lucy called out, waving to him from the pool.

He grimaced at me and put a tentative toe in the water. He swallowed hard. He didn't want to look a wimp in front of Lucy.

"The water is lovely," Lucy said, swimming to the edge.

Someone charged past and Wolfie lost his balance. Arms and legs flailing, he fell into the water, with a big splash. It reminded him of the time he was at the caves. He closed his eyes and spluttered. He had swallowed some water. He managed to wade his way through the fairly deep water and reached the edge again. Clinging on for dear life, he admitted: "Lucy, I can't swim."

"Never mind, I'll teach you. I taught my brother to swim, too." She took him by the hand and showed him the basics. Wolfie watched her every move intently. The swimming teacher was busy with some of the other kids.

"You see, it's quite easy, once you get the hang of it."

Wolfie smiled bravely and tried a few strokes. He somehow managed to stay afloat for a few moments and felt proud of the fact.

"So when do you have to go home?" Lucy asked.

"I'm not sure when I will be sent for," he said, with a sigh. This wasn't a lie, as he really didn't know when they would be able to get in touch with Dr G and arrange for his transfer home. They had tried to contact Dr G via the Internet several times and still there was no sign of life in the caves. It was worrying Wolfie and he wondered if he would ever get back home and see his family again. "It could be any day."

Lucy's face fell. "I wish you could stay longer. It's a pity that you have to go back."

"I know." He didn't know what else to say. He knew that he would never see her again and the thought saddened him.

"Maybe we could keep in touch. We could write to each other." Her eyes lit up.

Wolfie gave a wry smile. He knew this was quite impossible, but he didn't want to upset Lucy, so he agreed.

"Maybe I could visit you when I go skiing next year," she went on.

"Yes, that would be nice." He gave a brave, but sad little smile.

He vowed to himself that he would write her a letter before he left, explaining everything.

Wolfie had almost forgotten about his dental appointment. Mum and I had taken him and here he was, in the dentist's waiting room, nervously drumming his fingers on the edge of the seat.

"My tooth is all right now, Mrs Walker. Really."

"It won't hurt, you know", she told him.

When his name was called out, he sat rigid with fear.

"It's your turn, just follow the nurse," she said soothingly. "There's absolutely nothing to worry about."

He cast a nervous glance into the treatment room, which had a huge chair, which looked like something out of Star Trek.

"Can you please come in with me?" he asked in a trembling voice. He looked around the room with large, curious eyes and cringed at the sight of the syringes. They looked awesome.

"It's his first time and he's a bit nervous," Mum explained to the nurse.

Wolfie sat down carefully in the space chair. Gripping the edges of the seat, he looked at the kindly nurse beside him.

"Relax, dear. Dr Payne won't hurt you. You'll probably just need a little filling, don't worry."

"Filling? Are you—are you going to let my blood?" he managed to squeak.

"Let your blood what?" she asked, with a puzzled look on her face.

"You know—Apply leeches to suck my blood."

The nurse looked even more puzzled and shook her head. Before she could answer, Dr Payne arrived. "Right, then. Let's have a look at you. Open wide." Wolfie opened his mouth in a perfect little O-shape.

"No, wider than that." He looked and prodded around in Wolfie's mouth. "Aha, you need two fillings by the looks of it."

Wolfie held his head very still. The only things that moved were his eyes, large and frightened, when the nurse prepared an injection. He shut his eyes tightly and nearly fainted with fear at the sight of the needle coming towards him. There was a sharp sting. Tears rolled down his cheeks.

Within a few moments, his mouth was numb and he couldn't feel a thing. This made him relax a little, while the dentist prepared the drill, but it was short-lived. The noise of the drill was frightful and he trembled. "This won't hurt, dear," the nurse assured him, stroking his hand. He tried to pray, but his mouth was occupied with all sorts of objects and he couldn't even speak. The drill came closer and again, Wolfie shut his eyes so tightly that he was seeing stars on the inside of his eyelids.

"That's you ready, young man." He then turned to the nurse and whispered: "I've never seen anybody so frightened to get treatment. I thought he was going to pass out."

The nurse gave him a sticker. "Here you are. You deserve it." It read 'I was very brave at the dentist today', which he thought was a complete lie, as he had been a nervous wreck, fearing for his life, but that was beside the point.

Wolfie thanked him and the nurse and fled. His mouth felt all funny. It felt like it belonged to someone else. He touched it and it felt as though it was still stuffed with cotton wool. When he spoke, it felt funny too.

"He's done something to my mouth, it feels strange," he said when he got home. "Will it always be like this?"

"Course not, Wolfie," I assured him. "That's the anaesthetic, it will wear off soon." Poor Wolfie wasn't convinced. He sat looking at the clock, with a worried look on his face, as though he was counting the minutes. He held his cheek and there was a dribble of saliva coming from the corner of his mouth, as he had no feeling there. He wiped his mouth with his handkerchief.

"I can't give concerts dribbling like this. It's a sad situation", he muttered miserably. The anaesthetic wore off eventually, much to his relief. He became a bit chirpier after that. I told him he would be able to show off his fillings when he got home. He smiled and turned to look into the mirror with his mouth wide open. He touched the fillings.

"What an excellent idea, putting fillings in, and it didn't really hurt."

"We should have taken a photo of you at the dentist, just to show your parents," I told him.

"Talking of photos, I collected the ones we took at Wolfie's party. They came out really well," Mum said. "Apart from this one." She frowned and tucked it away.

We looked at them all and Wolfie was thrilled at having such lovely memories captured on photos.

"I've had extra copies made, so you can take these back with you," Mum said.

Tears sprang to his eyes. "Oh, thank you. Thank you so much." His voice was loaded with emotion. There were several photos with Lucy in them, so he was even more thrilled.

"In my era, people only get their portraits done by artists and no matter how good the artist is, it's never as real as these pictures are," he said.

We had a little laugh at the first photo ever taken of Wolfie, where he had got a shock when the flash went off. The result was a very funny photo where his face was contorted with shock, his mouth open and eyes wide in a grimace of fear.

We had a music lesson the next day. "This is more your cup of tea, as my Mum would say," I told him, as we piled into the music room.

There was a piano in the corner, which drew Wolfie like a magnet. He opened the lid and looked at the keyboard. He began to tinkle a little tune. He winced as he struck a key which produced a slightly out of tune note.

"It needs re-tuning," he told Neil and me.

"You're right", Mrs Grant, who had come in behind us, said in wonder.

"The tuner is coming on Friday." She deposited her music books on her desk and faced him. "So you are Wolfgang. I've heard a lot about you. Quite a musician, they say."

Wolfie smiled. "Well—" he said, with a nod of the head and a shrug.

"Maybe you could play us a tune," she went on eagerly. "To show us what they teach you in Austrian schools these days." She pushed her spectacles further up her nose.

"Yes, go on, Wolfie," Lucy urged.

Wolfie seemed to have no choice, so he happily went to sit down at the piano and played a tune by Bach. His hands floated swiftly over the piano keys and everyone listened, standing round in a large circle.

Mrs Grant was enthralled and clapped her hands when he stopped playing. "Outstanding. Not one mistake. Unbelievable," she exclaimed excitedly. "What is your tutor's name?"

"It's my father. He taught both my sister and me."

"He must be such a talented man. And you—you've got perfect pitch, it's so rare, it's—astonishing. Wolfgang, would you like to join the school orchestra?" she asked hopefully.

Wolfie hesitated. "Well, you see, I'm not here for long and—"

"Oh, but you simply must. They are practising for a concert," she stopped, disappointment clouding her face. "Oh but it's in two days' time, there won't be any time for you to practise, what a pity."

"What are they playing? I only have to hear it once and I'll remember it," Wolfie said keenly.

"Mozart's piano concerto in C major and other pieces," she said.

Wolfie smiled. It was on one of the CDs he had been given for his birthday. "I know it. It goes like this." He began to play it confidently.

Mrs Grant felt faint. She held onto the piano for support. "Remarkable," she said hoarsely. "You are a prodigy of nature. Can you stay after school to practise with the orchestra?"

Wolfie looked at me. I shrugged. "I'll call my parents to ask."

The rehearsal went well. There were children of all ages from primary to secondary school. Neil and I went along and sat in the theatre as they practised. Wolfie played the piano and later on the violin.

During the break, Mrs Grant said: "You are so talented Wolfie, just like your fellow countryman Mozart, who by a strange coincidence shares your first name, too."

Wolfie smiled. It felt odd that she was talking about him but didn't know it.

"He was by far the best composer ever, he had such versatility, he wrote so many symphonies, concertos, sonatas, church music, operas." She paused. "He was a musical genius."

Wolfie blushed.

"It is such a pity that he died so young," Mrs Grant said, shaking her head sadly.

Wolfie blanched. His mouth went dry. "What do you mean, he died young? How old was he?"

"He died in 1791, at the age of 35, with hardly any money to his name and nothing to show for his life, apart from a wealth of music."

Poor Wolfie felt sick with shock. He sank onto the nearest chair, the colour draining from his face.

"Wolfie, all you all right?" Mrs Grant said worriedly.

"He's not feeling well, he's very sensitive, you see," I said, wafting a music sheet over his face.

"Let's take him outside for some fresh air", Mrs Grant said, laying a hand on his clammy forehead. "The poor lamb, I hope he's not coming down with the flu."

I took him outside and sat him on a bench in the playground and Neil was sent to fetch a glass of water from the dining room.

"I'm all right now," he said faintly.

"You don't look it. Wolfie, I'm really sorry that you had to find out this way. I didn't want to tell you."

Wolfie took a deep breath and the colour returned to his cheeks. "That's why you told me to take care of myself and not to overdo things. You knew all the time."

"Yes, I did, but how could I possibly tell you?"

Tears stood in Wolfie's eyes. "Oh well, that's my dream gone. I thought I might be rich and famous and buy my parents a huge country house. Instead, I'll die young and penniless. Huh."

"Wolfie, you are immortal. Your music is immortal. Everything you write will be enjoyed for centuries to come, think of it that way," I said.

We hadn't heard the approaching footsteps, nor had we reckoned on Mrs Grant, Neil and various other kids overhearing our conversation.

I gasped, and put my hand over my mouth. "Oh, no."

Mrs Grant stood open-mouthed. "What—what exactly did you mean by that, Matthew? Wolfie is immortal? His music is immortal? Am I missing something here?"

Wolfie groaned and hid his face in his hands.

She sat down next to Wolfie. "Are you who I think you are? No it can't be. That's impossible. What is your full name? What is your date of birth?" she babbled on excitedly.

Resigned, he answered: "My name is Johannes Chrysostomus Wolfgang Theophilus," he paused and took a deep breath, "Mozart."

Chapter Fifteen

"I knew it, I knew it," Mrs Grant said with a hysterical edge to her voice.

"But how, how on earth did you manage to get here? A time machine?" she gave a shrill little laugh. "Has this got something to do with your disappearance, Matthew? Tell me." She laid her hand on Wolfie's shoulder.

"Mrs Grant, nobody is supposed to know. Please don't tell anyone," I pleaded. But from the look on her face and the excitement she showed it would be hard to keep her from telling anyone.

When we went back into the theatre to collect our things, there was a hushed silence as we walked in. They all stared at Wolfie as though he were an alien. It was obvious that they had all found out who he was.

We walked home. Wolfie's face was paler than usual and he walked along with his head down and his shoulders drooped. "Are you all right, Wolfie?" I asked. He nodded. "I suppose so."

Neil had a sulky expression on his face. "It's not fair, he burst out. "I've been your best friend for years. You've kept all this from me. We've never kept secrets from each other, before this."

"I know, and I'm sorry, but my Dad swore me to secrecy, I couldn't tell anyone, in case it all came out. Anyway I told you the whole story apart from the fact that Wolfie is who he is."

117

"I would have kept as quiet as a grave, you know that."

Wolfie paled even more at the word 'grave'. He stopped in his tracks. "Look, you two. I'm not deaf, you know. Stop talking about me as if I weren't here." It was the first time I had heard a note of irritation in Wolfie's voice. He was clearly very upset.

We told my parents what had happened. Dad was worried. "Who else knows?" he asked, pacing the living room floor.

"Well, there's Mrs Grant, Neil, some of the kids and they may have told the others."

Dad sighed. He puffed out his cheeks and then blew out. "Let's hope word doesn't get out then, it could turn the place into a circus."

Wolfie was in a quiet and wistful mood, prone to bursting into tears from time to time. He was sitting staring out of the sitting room window despondently. Mum tried to cheer him up.

"I bought some German sausage from the delicatessen shop, and look," she held up a jar. "Sauerkraut."

Wolfie tried a weak smile. "That's really thoughtful of you, Mrs Walker. You've been so good to me, so hospitable. I wish I could return the compliment, but I'm afraid I live rather far away."

"Wolfie, we are deeply honoured to have you staying with us. We're overjoyed about it."

Wolfie lifted his sad blue eyes to hers and said: "The honour is all mine."

"Now guess what's for dessert," she said cheerfully.

He shook his head. "Ice cream?"

"No, it's something you like. Matthew told me—apple strudel." She waited for his reaction.

He managed another faint smile. "That is my absolute favourite. Thank you very much."

Wolfie couldn't sleep that night. He tried hard, but was plagued by bad thoughts. He got up and tiptoed down the stairs. The steps creaked under his feet. It was a stormy night and outside the wind was howling. The eerie sound of an owl hooting into the empty darkness startled him. He looked out of the window. Shadows, made by tree branches bathed in street light, danced on the walls. He crept into the kitchen for a drink of milk, which he took through to the sitting room. He shut the door and switched on the lamp beside the book-case. He let his fingers trail over the books. It had to be here somewhere, he looked behind the books, and there it was, hidden at the back: 'The Life of Mozart'. He took a deep breath and carefully removed it from the shelf. He sank into the comfortable armchair with it and proceeded to read for almost two hours. His cheeks became flushed as his eyes devoured the pages of the book feverishly. When he read the truth about his life and early death, his eyes filled with tears. He would be famous, yes, especially in his youth. But in later years people would not value his true worth as a composer. He would die of a lingering illness. There would be no money for his funeral and his body would rest, along with several others, in an un-named grave. True fame would only come after his death.

With a sigh, he put the book down on the coffee table. No wonder they had concealed the truth from him. Silently he wept, head in hands. He felt so miserable and forlorn.

Mum came down in the morning and found him, finally asleep, in the armchair. They had a little chat and she gave him a comforting hug.

Lucy approached him in the playground that morning. "Is it true? Are you who they say you are?" She looked at his face intently, with bated breath.

"Yes, I am." He spread his hands. "I am Wolfgang Amadeus Mozart."

She exhaled. "Gosh, that's hard to take in. I suppose it explains a few things about you, like when you didn't know who Hitler was."

"Yes, I suppose it does." He gave a little smile.

"Does that mean that I won't ever see you again, when you go home?" she asked, in a small voice.

"Yes. My dear Lucy, I don't even know how I got here, how Matthew and I ended up in the caves. Modern technology, they tell me. Some sort of time machine Dr Gildenstein invented." He gave a shrug. "I was going to write you a letter before I left to try and explain."

The school bell summoned us in.

There was a bit of a commotion in the classroom when Wolfie and I walked in. All the kids crowded around us, as though Wolfie were an exhibit in a zoo. "Errr, excuse me, can you just let him get on with things, please?" I asked.

"So how did you get here? Was it a time machine? How will you get back home?" were some of the questions fires at him.

Miss Jennings looked at him differently too, but acted as if she was not entirely convinced about the story. Mrs Grant was with her.

"Master Mozart, will you still be able to take part in the concert tonight?" she asked, in a hopeful voice.

"I should very much like to, Mrs Grant." He was in a better frame of mind today. Mum's little chat seemed to have done the trick and he was optimistic again.

"Excellent," she shrieked, clapping her hands together. "Excellent." She turned and bumped clumsily into a desk.

The school day went much as usual, but during break time the kids were curious and bombarded them with questions.

"The whole school knows," I said to Dad.

"Hard to avoid, I suppose. Oh well, we tried our best to keep it a secret, didn't we. It can't be helped."

Wolfie was in a brighter mood. He was looking forward to the concert. He had decided, as everyone now knew who he was, to dress in his own clothes. He looked handsome and princely in his outfit.

The theatre was full. Wolfie was thrilled to be able to play for an audience again.

Mrs Grant gasped as he walked into the dressing room. "Oh, my dear. You look absolutely splendid. Are these the clothes you arrived here in? What a lovely wig, too." All the other young musicians were friendly and very respectful of Wolfie. Lucy popped in to wish him luck. She too, was stunned to see him in his own clothes. He bowed to her with a flourish and kissed her hand.

"My, you do look handsome, Wolfie," she breathed.

There were gasps from the audience when they saw Wolfie in his own clothes. He looked every inch an 18th century musician.

The concert was a great success. The young musicians were thrilled to be able to play with such a distinguished composer. Lots of people took photos of Wolfie and the rest of the school orchestra members.

The next morning we were dashing about getting ready for school. When the doorbell went Mum called out: "Can one of you boys get that, please, I'm still in my dressing gown. It's probably the milkman." She spoke through clenched teeth, as she had one of her face packs on. This one was green. I had warned Wolfie about Mum's face packs, should he come across her one day and get a fright.

"I'll get it," Wolfie called out. He cheerfully opened the door to be met by a barrage of people armed with cameras, smiles and questions.

"Are you really Wolfgang Mozart? How did you get here? Tell us your story. What are your plans? Will you give more concerts? What's your favourite breakfast cereal? What shoe size do you take?" were some of the questions that were fired at him. Photographers snapped their cameras, sounding like crocodiles' snapping teeth. Wolfie gulped and blinked hard, then shut the door. He looked through the window to check if he hadn't been dreaming. No, they were still there all right. They rang the bell again, insistently this time.

Mum came to see what the commotion was. She had completely forgotten about her face pack, as she opened the door. "No, don't open it," Wolfie warned her.

"Click click click," went the photographers. Mum shrieked, and banged the door shut.

"My worst nightmare has come true," she said, with a shudder. "I hope they don't print those pictures. She sympathised with the Prime Minister's wife Cherie Blair, who had been caught out by the press when she opened the door in her nightgown the day after the election. Dad was horrified. "They're just like vultures. I wonder what they'll make of this."

The press camped on the doorstep all day, ringing the doorbell constantly, until Dad took the batteries out, then they started banging on the door.

"Maybe I should answer their questions, what do you think?" Wolfie offered.

"No, you'd better to stay put. They'll get fed up and leave soon."

The evening papers' headlines read: *'Wunderkind Wolfgang alive and well,'* and: *'Mozart—reincarnated or the real thing?'* and' *'Musical genius living in London suburb.'*

The front page had a photo of Wolfie opening the door, and when they opened the paper, there was one of Mum in her hideous face pack, with a grimace of shock.

"That's it. I'll never be able to show my face outside the door again," she wailed. She held her head in her hands.

"Don't be silly dear, no one would recognise you," Dad offered. "Not without your face pack anyway."

We couldn't suppress our sniggers. Needless to say, she hasn't used a face pack since that day.

The next morning, the national newspapers were full of stories about Wolfie.

Dad had managed to sneak out of the back door to buy the papers. The headlines screamed: *'Is Mozart an alien?'* and: *'Phenomenon: Is musical genius really 250 years old?'* and: *'Is Mozart the son of God?'*

"Just as I had expected, it's turned into a circus", Dad announced.

Wolfie took a sip of tea and opened one of the newspapers, which said that he was an alien, and upon glancing at page three, he spluttered out his mouthful of tea. He hastily closed the paper, blushing furiously.

"There's a lady with no clothes on in here," he said, in a shocked voice.

I took a look. "Yes, that's a page three girl," I told him.

"But—but—she's displaying her bosoms," he uttered, with distaste.

"I know. It's positively indecent," Dad agreed, with a look of mock-horror on his face.

It took poor Wolfie a while to get over the shock of it.

There was a story in one of the papers, which told of Wolfie's visit to the British Library. The curator said that he had overheard him say that it was his motet, then he had checked his likeness in the portraits and that the boy definitely was Mozart.

The phone never stopped ringing with offers for exclusive interviews and TV chat shows. "Maybe you should hold a press conference, then they'll maybe leave you alone," Mum suggested.

"Yes, I had wanted to avoid that for your own safety, but it looks like that's the only solution," Dad agreed.

We arranged for a press conference in a local hotel the following day. Hundreds of reporters turned up,

"You see how famous you've become, Wolfie," I told him.

Hundreds of questions were fired. Wolfie tried to reply to them as best as he could, and told them of his plans. He seemed to be lapping it all up and was clearly used to a lot of attention. "Will you be giving more concerts, Master Mozart?" someone asks.

Wolfie mused. A slow smile spread over his face. "Perhaps."

That evening we checked the web-cam on the Internet again.

The screen was darkened by a cloud of smoke and, as we watched, there were fierce tremors, like a stampede of horses, then a huge explosion, which hurled burning rocks into the sky. Horrified, I said: "Oh, my God, the volcano has erupted." We looked on helplessly as the lava spread, filling the caves. The angry volcano roared again, sending rivers of lava down its slopes, darkening the atmosphere and spewing ash-laden smoke into the sky.

"I hope they got out in time," Wolfie remarked, in a shaky voice.

"Yes," I agreed, still reeling at what we had witnessed.

Wolfie was resigned to the fact that he would probably never be able to return home.

He was saddened, but a part of him told him that someone else would probably invent a transporter and then he would be able to go back to his family.

In the meantime, he kept himself busy by composing various sonatas and a symphony.
He looked forward to giving more concerts.

Chapter Sixteen

Within the next few weeks, Wolfie was giving concerts all over London and enjoyed his success immensely. He made recordings and reached No 1 in the charts, resulting in an appearance on Top of the Pops. He was in his glory. He was on TV, on chat shows, radio shows, he played in the Albert Hall, and all the grand concert halls in London. He earned pots of money, too, which he loved spending. He had a very generous nature, and when he went on his spending sprees he bought us all presents. He bought some smart outfits for himself for his concerts, but people preferred to see him in his own outfit.

"Aah, I could get used to this," he said, when he was stopped in the street for autographs, before entering the Albert Hall for his sell-out concert.

We got a nice surprise when we saw Dr Gildenstein, who turned up at the end of the concert. He was standing outside the dressing room.

I spotted him first. "Dr G. You're alive. Where have you been? We thought you had died in the volcano eruption. We saw it on the website."

Wolfie was thrilled to see him, too. He hugged him. "Thank God that you're alive."

"What happened?"

Dr G began: "After I transported you back home, Matthew, the volcano began its worst rumblings and we had to get the transporter out of the caves immediately, so I arranged for a van to collect it. It got damaged in transit and the machine malfunctioned. Luckily I managed to repair it.

Because of the haste of the situation, I didn't realise that Wolfie had been transported back with you and it was only afterwards, when I read the newspapers, I realised that he was here. I was jolly surprised, I can tell you.

"So what happened to Diabolus and Spike? Did they get out in time, too?" I asked him.

"Yes, they are safe. They're in London. In fact, they want to speak to you. Diabolus realises that he did wrong by kidnapping you both and he feels really bad about it."

"Really? He must have had a change of heart then," I said.

"That's not all, guess who's back with them?"

"Who?" we asked in unison.

"Spike's Mum. We managed to retrieve her from that nasty situation she found herself in."

"Goodness. How?" Wolfie asked.

"I set the transporter to the time before the first eruption of the volcano, when she was still alive, and we got her out of there, before her fate was sealed.

"How incredible," I gasped. "You have invented a marvellous machine, Dr G. Such an advance on modern technology," I said.

"Well, strictly speaking, we have been working on this for hundreds of years, you know."

"Since my time?" Wolfie asked.

Dr G chuckled. "No", he shook his head. "I may as well tell you, boys. I'm not from this millennium either. I'm from the year 3030."

It was our turn to be totally dumbstruck. "You are from the future? That is fantastic. You will know so much about future technology. Oh, please tell us more."

"But no-one must know about the transporter. People would make great misuse of it. Diabolus has learned his lesson the hard way. He was greedy for money and it all went wrong. Can I trust you boys?"

"Of course you can."

"Let me know when you want to go home, Wolfie". "I realise that you have a few more concert dates this weekend. Make the most of them. Enjoy it while it lasts.

"Yes, I will. I can't wait to see my family again. I have made so much money here, it'll last for years. They will be so pleased."

As Wolfie would not be able to use the money in his century, we had gone out with Dad and bought lots of gold and jewels with it, which could then be sold in Salzburg. He also bought a stack of whoopee cushions in the joke shop, among other fun items to surprise his family with.

Diabolus, his wife, and Spike came to visit us, accompanied by Dr G. I didn't recognise him at first. He actually looked human, clean-shaven and his hair had been cut. He wore a suit and looked very respectable. Spike looked equally normal, too. Gone was the green Mohican hairstyle, gone was the safety pin in his nose, making way for quite a presentable individual.

His wife Martha was pleased to meet us. Her serene face was now animated and expressive, no longer the sad expression on the grey statue we remembered.

"Archie has something to say to you both."

"Archie?" I asked.

"Yes, his real name is Archie Winterbottom," Martha explained. "Diabolus was his stage name when he used to be a hypnotist."

He stared at the floor, shame-faced, then he lifted his face to us.

Clearing his throat first, he said: "I truly am very sorry for kidnapping you and being so nasty to you boys. Will you forgive me?"

"Yes, of course, Mr—um—Winterbottom," I said, speaking for both of us. Wolfie nodded vigorously. I noticed that he was holding his breath, and going red in the face. He obviously found the name very amusing and if I had tried to make him speak, his giggle would have erupted, somehow spoiling the effect of our acceptance of his apology.

He shook hands with us both. I noticed that his nails had been cut and looked clean.

When the time came to say goodbye, both my parents came along, not wishing to take any chances this time. We went to Diabolus' house, where he had placed the transporter.

"Wolfie, once you get back, you will remember your adventure, but the future will automatically be erased from your memory," Dr G told him.

"I am pleased about that. I'd rather not know what lies in front of me once I get back." He gave a wry smile.

He had already said an emotional farewell to Lucy, which had almost reduced him to tears. Then he had gathered all his belongings in a large suitcase, which weighed a ton. "Before I go, I want you to have this," Wolfie said, handing me his violin.

Shocked, I said: "No, I couldn't accept that, Wolfie. It's so precious."

"Please take it. I have another one at home, besides, I will be able to get a new one," he insisted. "I shall feel hurt if you don't accept it."

I hesitated, then stepped forward to take it. "Thank you very much. I'll always take very good care of it, I promise." Tears pricked my eyes.

"Litt ew teem niaga," Wolfie said.

I translated it slowly. "Till—we—meet—again."

"You bet," I told him.

He hugged my Mum and Dad. He then thanked Dr G.

"I shall miss you all. Thank you very much for your hospitality." He swallowed the lump in his throat.

"Please give my best wishes to your parents and Nannerl."

"Now make sure that you don't touch each other when I press the exchange button," Dr G said, with a broad smile. "Otherwise it will be like musical centuries."

I laughed, but felt tears welling up in my eyes. Wolfie gave me a bear hug.

"Goodbye, my friend." He entered the cabin, taking a last look at us, before shutting the door. I gave him a little wave.

"Good luck, Wolfie."

He raised a hand in farewell and with a 'zap' and a 'bang' he was back where he belonged.

I felt a sense of loss. Wolfie had been such good company for the last few weeks. It would feel very strange without him.

Mum put a consoling hand on my arm. "Come on, time to go home." Her eyes looked red, as though she'd been crying.

Dad sighed. "Well, at least he's safely home now. Back where he belongs, with his family."

I sat in my room and picked up Wolfie's violin. I played the tune that he had dedicated to me and I felt a great surge of pride. Thoughts milled around in my head, as I went over my adventure. I could still hear his silly giggle.

Then Mum's voice brought me back to the present. "Matthew, it's teatime," she called out. I smiled. Life would go on, just like it always had. The good thing was, I had learnt a lot of things in the last few weeks.

Thanks to Wolfie and my trip to Salzburg, I had managed to finish my history project, with enthusiasm, I may add. I was able to authentically describe life in the 18th century with real vividness, having had the privilege of visiting it. Oh yes, and I got top marks for it.

I still play on my computer a lot, but I am very careful these days, when I log onto the Internet. You never know what lurks behind the screen.

There's Mum calling again. I'd better go downstairs. Star Trek is on soon and I don't want to miss it.

Printed in the United States
76432LV00009B/9